LOST AND FOUND

ALSO BY DAWN CHALKER

Bear Me in Mind
Where's the Vacation?

Lost and Found

A Novel

Dawn Chalker

Hepatica Books

Cover design by Briana Chalker and Peter Solenberger
Author photo by Briana Chalker

Library of Congress Control Number: 2024927074
ISBN 979-8-9922607-0-0

Hepatica Books
Traverse City, Michigan
hepaticabooks.com

For my sister Charlene Chalker Brinkert,
who is very much missed.

I'll be seeing you
In all the old familiar places
That this heart of mine embraces
All day through.
— Billie Holiday, "I'll Be Seeing You"
(Composed by Sammy Fain and Irving Kahal)

One

Summer 2023

Maria stands by the hospital bed and watches her grandmother sleep. Her face is pale and to Maria she looks shrunken. At least her grandma seems more peaceful now than she did when she had the stroke. Maria had felt so frightened as she tapped 911. Will her grandma recover? What will happen to Maria if she does not? Without her mother and sister, her grandma is all the family she has.

She needs to find somewhere to stay. Her body hums with the insistent feeling that she has to leave ASAP. She is definitely not going into foster care. A girl who sat next to her in seventh-grade English class was put into foster care, and a week later, the teacher said the girl had gone to stay with a family in another town. The class never saw her again.

Her grandmother's neighbor, Mrs. Porter, tells the nurse that she is leaving and will check back to see how Grandma is doing in a couple of days. Maria follows Mrs. Porter out of the room so it will look like she is going home with Grandma's neighbor. All the way down the corridor, Mrs. Porter keeps up a steady chat.

"Your grandma is a strong woman and will come through this. When my own mother had a stroke, she mostly recovered. Medical science can do wonders, you know." Maria barely hears her.

At the end of the corridor, Mrs. Porter stops walking and pats Maria on the arm. "Now, you call me if you or your grandmother need anything. And don't you worry. Your grandmother will ask the social worker to find someone for you to stay with while she recovers. Those people who take in young people are really great, I hear."

Maria shivers. She looks toward the stairway exit. "Guess I'll go down to the snack bar while Grandma is asleep."

"Yes, you should eat. You've got to keep up your strength." Maria nods and raises a limp hand in goodbye as Mrs. Porter walks away.

From the door to the stairs, she watches Mrs. Porter get on the elevator at the other end of the hall. Maria scurries down the stairs to the main level of the hospital. At the bottom of the stairs, she leaves the hospital by a side door. It is a relief to breathe the fresh air after the antiseptic smell of the hospital.

She looks in all directions to make sure no one notices her. Although she doesn't really know many people here anyway. The streets are mostly quiet. Two cars drive out of the parking structure. Three people walk briskly up to the hospital entrance and enter the front door.

Hurrying the few blocks to her grandmother's house, she thinks about the bus trips around the peninsula that she took with her grandmother. She remembers all the small towns they rode through on the bus. Another time her grandma's neighbors took them hiking on the old farm trail. She could get off in Empire and walk the rest of the way to safety.

Pulling items from her bedroom dresser, she stuffs extra clothes into her backpack. She picks up the photo of herself and her sister standing with her mom, her mom's arms draped around both of them, and packs it among the clothes. From the bathroom, she grabs her toothbrush and a few other things she might need.

In the kitchen she takes a couple of apples, an orange, and a chunk of cheese from the refrigerator. She picks up the half-loaf of bread from the counter and a few granola bars from the cupboard, then fills two water bottles. She stows the food and water in a plastic bag and stuffs it in the backpack. From the side table in the living room, she picks up the fantasy book that she was reading earlier. It's a library book, and she hopes it isn't due soon. She puts on the hoodie she had flung across the chair last night.

Locking the front door from inside, she walks out the back door. Lorena and Manuel who live in the house next door left yesterday to visit their daughter in Chicago. Her grandmother is closer to them than anyone else in town because they used to live in Mexico, and she speaks Spanish with them. If they were here, they would definitely visit her grandmother in the hospital and ask about Maria. Since they are not around, they will not tell her grandmother that she is not staying with Mrs. Porter or anyone else.

Maria sneaks through their backyard to take a shortcut to the next street over. Bruno, their dog, went on vacation with them, so he will not let out his deep woof. Just me, she usually calls out to him. Bruno sounds tough, but he's a pushover for a bit of attention. She wishes she could take him with her for company.

As she starts down the street, she starts to breathe more rapidly. Can she do this? She stops suddenly. Maybe she should just go back to the house. In her pocket she curls her fingers around the small wooden blue cat with the rainbow-striped body that her mother gave her when she told her to be brave. Her mom and sister are brave. She has to do this.

Walking another few blocks, she crosses the street to the bus stop on the bay side of the road. While she waits for the bus, she pulls up her hood, turns her back to the busy road, and watches white-capped waves roll into the beach along the shore in front of her. A three-masted ship gusts across the bay in a brisk wind. She fingers the bus card in her pocket that her grandma had given her so she could ride a bus to the library or downtown.

A group of teenage girls saunter down the street towards her, talking and laughing loudly. She steps off the sidewalk and waits for them to pass by. She doesn't know any of them, and that makes her feel even more lonely.

The whoosh of the bus startles her as it stops behind her. She keeps her head down and slides into the empty seat in the second row from the front. To discourage anyone from sitting next to her, she sets her backpack on the seat.

Out the window she sees a police car passing the bus. Has someone sent the cops after her? Her body stiffens. The car zooms on by and she lets out her breath.

The ride to Empire takes longer than she expected, with several stops along the way. Each time the bus stops, she scrunches down on the seat and looks out the window. The bus whizzes past several storage areas, a showcase where people can buy boats, and a gas station that sells pizza. Farther from town there are a couple of farms and a horse ranch.

She turns her head and looks back, not sure what she saw. A life-sized copper-colored metal T-Rex stands in a field flanked by two large metal butterflies. Funny.

As she watches the intense green trees lined up along the side of the road flash by, she wonders if she is making the right decision. Should she call her friend in Ann Arbor and see if she could stay with her family? But her grandmother will need her here, if she gets well again. IF, the Big IF. She tamps down her fears and congratulates herself for making her escape.

In Empire she gets off the bus and walks along the highway. A couple of cars pass by, and she moves farther off the road. A car stops beside her and a man rolls down the window.

"Hey, need a ride?" He smiles and gestures to the passenger seat of the car.

Maria's eyes grow wide and she clenches her hands. She vigorously shakes her head and quickens her pace with her head down.

"Suit yourself." The car pulls away.

The thought of being forced into a stranger's car makes her jittery. She wipes tears from her eyes and stays near the edge of the trees. A gentle breeze riffles the leaves, and she glimpses a few flowers farther back in the woods. The distance seemed shorter when she was in the car with her grandmother. She lifts her shoulders to ease the feel of the backpack and trudges on.

Following a curve in the highway, she turns right onto the road that will take her to her destination and breathes more easily. Farther down where the paving ends, she spots two cars parked along the side of the road. With her backpack, she will just look like another hiker. She straightens her shoulders and steps around the barrier onto the trail.

Two

Tara parks her car on the side of the road near the trailhead behind the two cars that are already there. Taffy jumps out of the backseat when Tara opens the door.

"You can run off leash for a while. Not many people here today."

Tall trees provide a bright green canopy as their leaves sway gently in the breeze. Brown leaves from the previous fall crunch underneath Tara's feet as she walks briskly along the wide path. Yellow bellwort flowers growing beside the trail nod on their tall stems. Among them, pink and yellow columbine flowers brighten the edges of the path.

Taffy trots along beside Tara. "Looks like we missed the trillium. Just a few still hanging on. That was Aunt Becca's favorite wildflower." The dog darts off the trail and Tara watches her weave through the trees, patches of white and caramel flash through the grass and flowers.

At the top of a small hill, she breathes in the tangy scent of the pines and the sweet-smelling ferns that unfurl throughout the woods. A few starflowers catch her eye, their sharp star shape bright white among the frothier Canada mayflowers.

When she spots a couple walking towards her, she calls, "Come, Taffy." Taffy stops suddenly, runs back to Tara's side. She snaps on the dog's leash, and the dog prances beside her as the couple approaches.

"Nice day for a hike." The man smiles.

"Yes." Tara manages to smile back.

"Beautiful dog. Would she mind if I pet her?" The woman looks at Taffy.

"She would be okay with that."

The woman holds out the back of her hand and Taffy sniffs it. She wags her stub tail as the woman gently strokes the soft head and ears. The couple tells Tara to enjoy her hike and walks on down the trail. Tara lets Taffy off the leash again.

Tara thinks back to five months ago when she adopted Taffy from the Humane Society. Tara had closed her laptop after her third Zoom meeting of the day. The latest fundraising campaign was coming together but lacked the excitement of an in-person event. During the pandemic, she was lucky to be able to work from home, but being at home by herself so much was getting old.

She looked out the window. Not much of a view, just patches of brown grass where the snow had melted. A bit of blue sky peeked out from the clouds briefly, letting a bit of sunshine filter through. She thought back to one of the summers she had spent with Aunt Rebecca and Uncle Robb. Out in their backyard, she threw sticks for their dog, Blaze. He was a medium-sized brown and black dog of mixed parentage. When she was there, he had followed her around and lain by the side of her bed at night. She had loved that dog as if he were her own and was heartbroken when he died a few years later.

On her phone she looked up the number for the Humane Society and called. They had time for an appointment at 4:00 if she wanted to check out the dogs available for adoption. Great, she would be there.

The Humane Society was in a low, brick building next to a field and a couple of houses. Individual fenced-in kennels lined one side, each with an entrance to the inside of the building. Only a few cars sat in the parking lot. During Covid people weren't allowed to visit the animals whenever they felt like it. Appointments were required.

Tara took a couple of deep breaths. She had never adopted a dog before. On the form the receptionist handed her, she wrote her name and address and answered questions about her ability to care for a dog. A few minutes later, a staff member came around the reception counter.

"Hi, I'm Beth. You're Tara? Looking to adopt a dog?"

Tara nodded. Her hands felt clammy. What if they didn't think she was worthy of adopting a dog?

"Come on back. Just a few preliminary questions." Beth led her to a small office in the back of the reception area and gestured to a chair. Tara sat and Beth sat across from her.

"Why do you want to adopt a dog?" Beth leaned forward.

"For companionship. To take for walks. My aunt and uncle had a dog that I was very fond of. This seemed like a good time."

"We have had quite a few adoptions during the Pandemic. But some of those dogs ended up being returned. We are trying to be much clearer about the responsibility of adoption. What is your living arrangement?"

"I live in an apartment. But there is a park a block away where we can go for walks and a dog run a few blocks farther down."

"Does your lease allow for dogs?"

"Yes, if I pay an extra fee per month." Tara swallowed. Her mouth felt dry. She did not want to say that it would be a bit of a stretch to come up with the money. But she had figured out what things she would do without in order to pay the extra fee. "I checked my budget and it won't be a problem."

"Do you have roommates?"

"No, it's just me." It sounds sad to say that. She isn't used to living alone just yet.

"Well, let's go look at the dogs we have today who are in need of a good home."

Beth led her to the kennels where each dog had its own space with a pet door that opened to the small outdoor enclosures. Some of the dogs rushed to the front of their cages as people walked by.

For Tara, one dog stood out from all the rest, a brown and white Brittany Spaniel with eager, brown eyes. The dog came cautiously up to the fence, sat down, and looked up at Tara. She held one paw up to the fence as if she were reaching out to her. Tara looked up at the name plate on the fence.

"Taffy. The perfect name." Tara kneeled down, reached her fingers through the wire, touched Taffy's ear, and smiled. "Hello, would you like to go home with me?" The dog stood up and wagged her tail.

"Looks like the two of you have made a connection. Snap on her leash and take her for a walk around the grounds." Tara took the leash hanging by the cage door and snapped it onto Taffy's collar. "Want to go for a walk with me?" Taffy wagged her tail.

Tara followed Beth down the hall to the door leading out to a large, fenced-in area. "You two spend some time out here and I'll be back in a few." Beth went back inside.

Tara walked Taffy around the perimeter, staying a distance away from the other dogs walking with people. Taffy stuck close to her until they passed a man with two young children who petted a young black lab. Taffy's ears perked up, and she pulled on the leash to get closer to them. The two dogs checked each other out while the kids took turns petting both of them.

Tara chatted with the man for a few minutes and then she gently pulled Taffy away. "I guess you like kids." She patted Taffy on the head. After they made a circuit of the area, Tara sat down and leaned against the fence. Taffy laid down beside her. Tara continued to talk to the dog and stroke her soft fur.

Beth walked up to them and smiled. "Looks like success. Come back to my office, and let's talk about finalizing the adoption."

Tara and Taffy followed Beth back into the building and into her office.

"Taffy is one of those dogs who were returned to us. The father lost his job. The family did not want to part with her, but they could not afford to keep her. Taffy is sensitive. The first few days she was here, she lay with her head on her paws and a soulful look in her eyes. Eventually, she perked up a bit, and I have to say you are the first person she has rushed to greet. You need to be committed to her and reassure her that she is in her forever home. Are you prepared to take Taffy with you today?"

"Yes. And I will be sure she feels wanted. Except that I don't have a leash or dogfood. I know I sound unprepared, but I wasn't sure I would find the right dog. And Taffy is definitely the right one."

"We can send a collar, leash, and dog dishes home with you for a fee. And a small bag of the food Taffy eats here to get you started."

"Thanks. That would be great."

Beth finished the paperwork and walked Tara and Taffy out to the parking lot.

With a collar on and the leash and food provisions in the car, Tara took the dog home. For the first few days, Taffy followed her from room to room and slept beside her bed every night. Tara worked at home and spent her free time taking Taffy for walks, helping her get used to strangers, teaching her to come when she was called, and playing fetch, which became a favorite game for both of them.

At the top of the hill, Tara stops to admire the old farm house on the hill that overlooks a large field. Once a working farm, it was abandoned and taken over by the Park Service. Locals call it the old Spencer farm.

On the left is a weathered red wooden barn with a stone wall along one side of it. Tara sees where someone has replaced some of the old boards with newer ones. Next to the bottom of the hill is another low-roofed building, maybe for storage. To the right is an arched wooden door cut into the side of the hill, and Tara wonders what it was used for.

Taffy races ahead of Tara up the hill to the old farmhouse. A porch spans the front of the white, two-story house. A sign that says, "Please stay off the porch," hangs from a rope stretched between the porch posts. Some of the old steps have crumbled along their edges. The bay window on one side of the front provides views of the expansive field for someone to sit inside and watch the crops grow. The only furniture in the room is an old wooden table with three chairs.

Tara wishes that the house had been rehabbed by the Park Service so she could see how it might have looked when people lied here. She continues around the side of the house and looks in the window of a room that is empty except for a wooden rocking chair.

Taffy follows her to the back of the house. Tara walks up the steps of the back porch and peers through the cracked window at the top of the door. Must have been the kitchen. Along one side of the room is a deep sink with a hand pump. Beside it is an old wood-burning stove with a door big enough to insert large pieces of wood.

Taffy gently paws at the door and barks.

"What is it, Taff? Do you think a raccoon or skunk got inside? The house is locked so we can't check that out." Taffy continues to paw at the door and barks again. Tara gently takes hold of her collar and pulls her down off the porch.

"Come on, Taffy. I'll race you."

Taffy tears past her, around the house and down the trail to the bottom of the hill. Wagging her tail, she stops and waits for Tara to catch up.

Tara sits on the stone steps that lead up to the barn. She hears a song that sounds like a medley of songs of different birds coming from the same location. She listens again and follows the sound to the top of a tall tree where a lone bird sits, dark gray back with a light gray breast. She can just barely see white bars on its wings as it tips its head back to continue singing. Looks and sounds like a mockingbird. A treat she would love to share with her aunt, who was an expert at identifying bird songs.

When she was about ten, she and her aunt sat on these steps and told stories about a family who might have lived on the farm. Tara had imagined a large, happy family with five children. They raised all kinds of vegetables and took care of horses, cows, goats, sheep, several dogs and cats. The children in the family had adventures that included a treasure hunt through the woods where they found a chest of gold; saving a drowning family from a capsized boat; and being stranded in a huge snowstorm with snow piled up six feet outside their window. Her aunt always encouraged her imagination. Who would do that now?

Tara stands up and takes the trail across the field towards the bluff that overlooks Lake Michigan. As she passes the farmhouse from below, she looks toward the upper story. A shadow passes across the window, and she looks up at the sky, expecting to see a cloud scudding across. But the sky is still a brilliant, early summer blue. "Just a trick of the light, I guess." She looks back at the window but sees nothing.

On the field trail, Taffy runs back and forth, explores the field one minute and keeps track of Tara the next. On the bluff along Lake Michigan, Tara gazes out across the expanse of water. Gentle waves roll in from the deep navy blue of the water farther out to the shallow aqua water near the shore. The long sandy beach below the dune curves as far as she can see to the left and as far as she can see to the right. Two sets of footprints pressed into the wet sand mark a path along the shoreline.

Tara leans against a tree and thinks back. Did she make the right choice six months ago?

It was a gloomy January day. The sun hadn't shone for more than a few minutes a day for weeks it seemed. A big snowstorm had created huge piles of snow that turned to brown slush when the weather warmed up a bit.

Tara went into the kitchen and chopped vegetables, dumped them into small bowls. She stopped and poured herself a glass of wine. Kyle was supposed to be home an hour ago. She had gotten used to his late nights at work, but she was still annoyed that he never called to let her know that he would be late. She heard the front door open and then close. Kyle dropped his things on the table by the door and she heard his footsteps.

"Hi. You're fixing dinner."

Tara put down the knife and turned to look at him. He stood in the doorway, not coming into the kitchen.

"Course. We have to eat." She turned back to the vegetables. When did their relationship become so stilted? When had he stopped calling out that he was home and coming to hug and kiss her hello?

"Can I help?"

"Pour yourself a glass of wine. Check the rice and see if it's done."

Kyle poured the wine and opened the pot lid to look at the rice. "Almost, I think."

Tara dumped the vegetables into a pan with the chunks of chicken. Kyle still stood a few feet away from her. They both asked the usual questions about each other's day and then were quiet.

When the stir-fry was cooked, she dished up plates and set them on the table. Where to begin?

"Kyle," she said as Kyle said, "Tara." They looked at each other.

"What?" she said first.

"I've been offered a job in Texas. It looks really promising."

"Did they ask you for an interview?"

"Already did the interview."

Tara raised her eyebrows. "What do you mean you already did the interview? You never said."

"A couple weeks ago when I went to Texas on business."

"The job is in Texas? Why didn't you tell me about it?"

"I wanted to check it out, to be sure it was what I want."

"What about what I want?"

"When I get settled, you'll come out, look for jobs, or take some time off to figure out what you want to do. This job pays a lot more than I'm making now. You won't have to start working right away if you don't want to."

Tara stared at him. How could he make this decision without discussing it with her? Did she want to move to Texas? She didn't think so.

"I'll have to think about it. This is a big change,"

"Change can be for the better. We haven't exactly been happy for a while."

"You haven't said you are unhappy."

"No. Neither have you."

She had nothing to say to that.

A few weeks later, Kyle boxed up his belongings and said he would send for them when he got settled. He packed some clothes into a couple of suitcases and grabbed his laptop. At the airport they hugged and said an awkward see you in a couple of weeks.

Two weeks later, Tara walked through the apartment. She looked at the empty space where Kyle's things used to be. The second bedroom that they shared as an office now felt much larger. The bedroom closet had a gaping hole where his clothes used to hang.

Tara looks out at the expanse of water, brings her thoughts back to the present. What would she be doing now if she had moved to Texas with Kyle? Would she like living in Dallas? But she needed some time to think about it, to consider her options. So, Kyle moved without her.

Five months ago, he texted that he had settled into an apartment. She could come out and join him, if she wanted. But he did not say he missed her, or needed her there, or that he loved her. And the more she thought about it, the more she realized that she didn't miss him all that much. Maybe they had just stayed together out of habit, because it was comfortable. Still, she felt lonely without his presence in her life. She had simply texted back, "glad you're settled in." She got a couple of texts after that, telling her how he liked his job, how he was meeting "cool" people. And she realized the relationship was over.

And then her Aunt Becca died, the person who Tara felt knew her the best. If only she could talk to her aunt about what she should do next. Her aunt would have had something wise and helpful to say.

She shakes off these thoughts and takes a picture of the lake with her phone, texts it to her friend Amber with a message, "Solace for my sorrows."

A text comes back a few seconds later, "How poetic. Miss you. I'm here if you need to talk."

Tara responds, "Thanks for being there."

"Taffy, come." Tara looks around for the dog, but doesn't see her at first. What would she do if she lost Taffy? Taffy dashes down from the top of the bluff, stops, and nudges Tara's hand with her head.

"You're right. Time to stop remembering the past and get on with it."

Waves swish gently into the shore below. The of the sun sets lower on the horizon, casting a golden glimmer across the lake in the western sky.

"Let's start back to the car." She strokes Taffy's soft, furry head. As they walk past the abandoned farm buildings, Tara again looks up at the house. She shivers, feeling as if someone is watching her from an upstairs window. "Don't be ridiculous. The house is empty." She shakes her head and keeps walking.

As they near the end of the trail, they meet an older couple just starting out. Tara holds on to Taffy's collar and exchanges greetings with them. She lets Taffy into the back seat of the car and drives back towards town.

Three

Tara walks past the living room where her uncle sleeps in his chair by the window. She searches the refrigerator and the cupboards for something to fix for dinner. Looks like her uncle hasn't been to the grocery store very often since Aunt Becca died. She chops vegetables for a salad, boils a pot of water for pasta, opens a jar of tomato sauce with sausage, and shreds cheese.

"You've started dinner." Uncle Robb stands in the kitchen doorway and looks around, as if the place isn't familiar to him anymore. "Guess I fell asleep. I don't usually do that in the afternoon."

"No problem."

"What should I do?"

"You could set the table, if you want." She watches her uncle open the cupboard door and stand in front of it a few seconds.

He lifts out a stack of plates and begins to place them on the table. When he starts to lay a third place, he stops and stares at the chair where her aunt used to sit. The chair is empty. Tara places a tossed salad and the bowl of pasta and sauce on the table.

Uncle Robb eats quietly, and Tara tries to distract him by telling him about her hike. He nods but doesn't comment.

"I've seen lots of 'now hiring' signs in store windows and think I'll apply for a job. I should make some money while I am here this summer. Tourist season is just beginning, so a summer job should work out just right, for now. Are you okay with that?"

Uncle Robb nods. "You must be bored, sticking around the house with an old guy."

"Not a bit. Not such an old guy. I am happy to get to spend time with you."

"Kind of you to say so. It is great comfort to have you here."

Tara pats his shoulder as she gets up and takes dishes to the sink. Uncle Robb helps her clean up the kitchen and goes back to the living room. Tara gives him some space for a few minutes. Sometimes grief just needs to be experienced, allowed to exist.

Tara takes the bag of garbage outside and dumps it into the garbage can for tomorrow's pickup. Then she goes into the garage to find the extra garbage bags. The tools are lined up in an orderly fashion on a pegboard along the back wall. When she picks up the box of garbage bags from the worktable, she notices the cross-country skis leaning against the corner, her cross-country skis.

Tara remembers getting those skis the Christmas when she was ten. She woke up in the darkness of a winter morning at her aunt and uncle's house. Her mom and stepdad brought her here the day before to stay for a few days, and then they left to spend some time alone together. Aunt Rebecca and Uncle Robb had missed out on celebrating Christmas morning with Tara, because her family spent Christmas with her stepdad's family that year. Her aunt and uncle wanted to redo the whole Christmas morning thing with Tara that morning. Which was fine with her, because Christmas with her stepdad's family never really felt like Christmas. Besides, you can never have too many Christmas mornings. Well, maybe you could if it was every day or something.

Tara tiptoed into the hall and down the stairs. The door to her aunt and uncle's bedroom was still closed. A bit of moonlight glinted through the clouds and lit up the dimness of the living room. Feeling her way, she turned on the tree lights, which gleamed on the wrapped presents and a beautiful pair of white cross-country skis with red and blue stripes across the tips of them. Tara laid the skis beside each other on the carpet and slid her feet into the bindings. She picked up the ski poles and imagined she was zipping down a snow-covered trail, flashing by the trees that sparkled with snow in the winter sun. She couldn't wait.

After breakfast she carried her skis and poles down to the basement, where there was a large, carpeted space.

"A good place to learn how to cross-country ski without falling over. And your Aunt Becca can show you how to slow down for those times when you just can't miss going down a beautiful hill. She took downhill ski lessons in high school, so she's a pro."

"I don't know if I'd say I'm a pro." Her aunt laughed as she followed them downstairs. "But I do say I don't often fall."

Uncle Robb showed Tara how to snap her boots into the ski bindings, then put on his own skis, and slid one foot slowly forward and then the other. He nodded to Tara and she did the same.

"That's not hard."

"Try pushing just a bit faster, to get a rhythm going." Uncle Robb started off and she followed behind him from one end of the basement to the other. "Slide and glide, slide and glide. Though you can't get much of a glide on carpet."

"You're doing great." Aunt Rebecca smiled. "Time to go outside and try out the snow. Just take it slowly at first, until the glide comes easily."

Outside, soft flakes of snow sifted down all around them. The cold tang of the air felt fresh and crisp. They clamped on their skis and practiced the slide and glide around the house, back and forth across the backyard. Tara teetered a little with the first couple of glides, but then relaxed into it.

"You're a natural." Uncle Robb clapped, and Tara gave a bow without falling down.

"Now, let me show you how to slow down a bit going downhill." Aunt Rebecca demonstrated how to push out the backs of the skis until she made a V-shape with the front of the skis.

"Like this?" Tara pushed out the backs of her skis, but the fronts ended up crossed over each other, causing her to tip forward. She stood straight and picked up one ski carefully to straighten it out.

"Way to go!" Uncle Robb grinned at her. "On to a real trail to practice on."

Snow fell constantly those few days, and her uncle took her skiing every day. She learned how to ski down a small hill without falling down, going a bit faster each time. Finding her own rhythm thrilled her, the feel of the snow gliding under her skis. She felt she could ski for hours and never tire. When they came back, they sipped hot chocolate and ate cookies, and everything felt right with the world.

After she cleans up the kitchen, Tara talks her uncle into going for a walk. He used to hike with her aunt all the time, but he hasn't hiked since her death. They choose a street that meanders through a less familiar neighborhood where they will meet fewer sympathetic neighbors. It is nice to know that people care, but neither of them wants to talk about Aunt Rebecca's death just now.

The freezer is full of casseroles, cookies, and soups that friends brought to the house for her uncle after her aunt died. Tara left them there so her uncle could eat them after she moves back to her own life and he is alone again.

Tara links her arm with her uncle. "How are you doing?" Uncle Robb pats her hand. "I'm coping, I guess. Definitely better since you arrived. I appreciate you taking time out from your own life to help me out."

"You and Aunt Becca were there for me so many times when I needed a safe haven from the complex chaos of my family. I am happy to do the same for you."

Uncle Robb nods.

Back at the house, Uncle Robb tells Tara that he wants to clear out some old books. Tara wonders if he is avoiding clearing out Aunt Rebecca's belongings because it is too painful. It has been three weeks since her aunt's funeral. Maybe it is too soon. How soon is soon when you have shared a life with someone for almost fifty years?

"What are these? Uncle Robb?" Tara pushes aside the books she is sorting and pulls three spiral notebooks off the bookshelf, one blue, one orange and one red.

"Uncle Robb?" she says again. She waits for him to come back from whatever memory of her aunt he has been musing on.

He looks over at her. "What's that?"

"These notebooks." She holds them up. "They look like they are from a long time ago."

He gives her a wan smile. "Your aunt brought them back from France, I think, and put them there."

"From France. Huh." Tara opens the blue one to the first page and reads 25 Janvier 1971 written at the top. She studied Spanish in high school, and she took one semester of

French in college, so she knows that Janvier means January. "Looks like a journal. 1971. Aunt Becca would have turned 21 that year. Have you read any of it?"

"No, I would never read your aunt's private writings."

"You were never tempted?"

Uncle Robb shakes his head. "We always respected each other's privacy."

"Did she talk much about France?"

"Some. Actually, I met her not long after she had returned to the States. And she told me a bit about her time there."

"How did you meet her?" Her aunt had once told her how they met, but she wanted to give her uncle a chance to talk about Aunt Becca. Besides, she had never heard his take on the story.

"I was walking down Vine Street in Kalamazoo, watching the sun create patterns on the sidewalk through the colored leaves of the trees. Out of the corner of my eye, I saw this girl — woman I should say now, I guess — sitting on the porch of a small, brick apartment building. She rested her chin on one hand. I thought she looked really sad. I slowed down and she looked up at me. She had big brown eyes, kind of teary brown eyes. I couldn't just walk by. So, I took a chance and said, 'Hi, you okay?'

"She looked at me a few seconds, then shook her head. Then I asked her if she lived there, had roommates. I didn't like to think of her sad and sitting there all alone. Your aunt was very beautiful, you know."

Tara smiles. "I know." Uncle Robb always thought Aunt Rebecca was beautiful, even as she got older and her hair started to turn silver gray.

"Well, she gestured to the door behind her indicating she lived there and said, 'Three roommates. Two off for the weekend and one at the library.'

"Without thinking, I walked over and asked if I could sit down beside her. She looked at me, like she was sizing me up. I thought she might tell me to leave her alone, but she nodded. We sat in silence for a minute and then I said I sometimes liked to sit outside and think about things. I talked about inconsequential things, told her a little about the classes I was taking.

"And then slowly she started to talk about leaving some guy behind in France and coming home. I think she was in love with him. And how the guy who was her boyfriend here before she went to France for six months had just broken up with her. He told her she was not the same since she came home, and she knew he was right about that. She would never be the same. I told her I thought it made sense that she would not be the same, and she gave me a weak smile.

"I said that must be tough. She shrugged and then began asking me more about myself. We talked for a while. I did not want our conversation to end, so I suggested that we get dinner at a natural foods cafe that had opened down the street."

"Very romantic." Tara smiles. "A connection. What everyone is looking for, I guess."

"We were both graduating that spring and felt uncertain about our futures."

"You both figured things out."

"True. Meeting your aunt was the best thing that ever happened to me." Uncle Robb gave a sad smile.

"She was pretty special. Did you get together after that?"

"No, I was an idiot. I was dating a woman and thought I should figure that out before I got involved with someone else. And, your aunt seemed vulnerable. I didn't want to be the rebound guy. Then I saw her on campus from across the street. She was with some guy, and they were talking intently. I figured she had found someone else, and regretted I had missed my chance."

"But you got together eventually."

Uncle Robb nods. Tara can see that he is tired, and talking about Aunt Becca has reminded him that she is gone.

"Mind if I keep these for a while? Do you think Aunt Rebecca would mind if I looked at them?"

"I don't think she would mind. She would do anything for you."

Tara nods. And grief at losing her aunt rolls over her again like a giant wave. When she was growing up, she knew her parents loved her when they got divorced. Although for a while she thought maybe she had done something to make them split up. Both of them remarried and started second families. Her step-brother and half-sisters are an important part of her family, but she never quite feels like she belongs.

Aunt Rebecca was ten years older than Tara's mom. Since she and Uncle Robb had no children of their own, they unofficially adopted Tara. She spent a lot of time at their house and even went on vacations with them. No one would love her as unconditionally as her aunt had.

Her uncle abandons the book sorting and sits in his chair, looking out the window. Tara lays down the journals. She thinks about her aunt coming home from France and feeling that she didn't quite fit into her own life anymore.

In high school Tara thought she would get a degree in music, play in an orchestra. She was first chair clarinet in the school orchestra and had gotten a first at the Solo and Ensemble Festival in her senior year. But after her first audition for a place in a university music program, she realized professional music was not for her. She could not imagine her life being full of auditions and rejections. And talking to music students, she heard how intense the music program was.

She wanted her university experience to be broader than constant practicing and trying to please sometimes difficult professors. She didn't really want to end up teaching music in a school, like some of her music friends planned to do.

When she graduated from the University of Michigan, she felt disoriented, unsure what she wanted to do. For five years she had focused on getting her college degree, but she didn't know what to do next. A BS with a major in English and a minor in Ecology didn't translate into anything very specific, perhaps not a very smart choice of a combination. Everyone said to do what you love, but that didn't mean you would get a job doing it.

A friend told her about a job opening as an event organizer, fundraising for a non-profit organization. They needed someone right away to help organize a big event coming up soon. She applied for the job, was hired, and worked there for five years. It was an okay job, but not really what she wanted to do for the rest of her life.

During the pandemic, the fundraising for in-person events dwindled, and she worked only part time. After Kyle left, she was barely able to pay the rent on her tiny apartment. Going back to live at her mom's house or her dad's house was not an option. Now that the pandemic has eased, events would begin to increase, but she needed a new plan for her life.

After Aunt Rebecca died of cancer, her mother suggested Tara move in with Uncle Robb. She thought Uncle Robb was feeling lost and wasn't taking good care of himself, but she still had a full-time job and didn't have time to look out for him.

Tara always loved staying with her aunt and uncle, so she agreed to move in with him for a while. It would give her time to think about what next. She gave two weeks' notice at her job and then moved, storing most of her things in Uncle Robb's basement.

She looks over at her uncle, who stares at an open book on his lap that she thinks he is not reading.

"Uncle Robb," she says softly. "Why don't you go to bed? It has been a long day." She puts her hand on his shoulder. He opens his eyes and looks up at her with tears in his eyes.

Tara sits beside him and takes his hand. It feels cool and rough from working outside.

"Just remembering Becca and the last time she spoke to me."

"Tell me."

"She had a restless night, but seemed more relaxed the next morning. She looked up at me and smiled. I was holding her hand and she squeezed it. She told me she loved me and what a good life we had had together. I could barely speak enough to tell her she was always the love of my life.

"She closed her eyes and fell asleep. I sat beside her for hours, hoping she would wake up again. I must have dozed off, because I jolted awake suddenly. And I knew. She was gone." He begins to cry.

Tara's voice chokes up but she manages to say, "I'm sorry. She was a very special person and I will always miss her."

"It was the worst moment of my life, to realize that she really was gone, never to return." His voice sounds hoarse and he wipes the tears from his eyes.

"Thanks." He eases out of his chair, thanks her for making dinner and for helping him, says good night, and climbs up the stairs to bed.

Tara sighs. She doesn't know what it would feel like to have lived with the same person, loved the same person, for so many years, and suddenly have them not be with you any longer.

Tara picks up the journals and goes upstairs. She gets ready for bed, picks up the blue notebook, and leans back against the pillows on her bed. Why did her aunt not talk much about the time she spent in France? Tara thought she knew most everything about her aunt, because her aunt loved to tell stories about her past. Not France, though. Although she credits her aunt's occasional use of French phrases with inspiring her to take a French class.

Tara smiles at the memory. Sitting at the desk in her room, she opens her laptop to catch up on her emails and the news. The Supreme Court has overturned the use of affirmative action in college admissions and sided with a web designer who refused service for gay weddings. Both of these decisions shock Tara. Like Roe v. Wade that was also overturned by the Supreme Court, she took affirmative action and equal rights for gay people as a given. It took a long time for women's rights and LGBTQ rights to be recognized. Do people have to start all over?

She closes her laptop and opens the journal that started the journey of her aunt to France.

Four

Paris, France
1971

Lundi, 25 Janvier

Well, I finally made it to France! It was a long overnight flight on a Jumbo jet in which they added extra seats. The International Airport at La Guardia was really crowded. Many people seemed to be leaving for Germany or Vietnam. When I left home, I was really sad, especially saying goodbye to Brian. But in the airport, I started to feel excited about starting on this big adventure. It was a big hassle getting my luggage from the domestic airport to the international one. I've never done anything like this before. Never taken luggage on a plane before!

During my long wait to board the plane to Paris, I met a girl named Marybeth from Denver. We found seats together next to Greg, a boy from New York City. Marybeth fell asleep halfway to France (over the Atlantic Ocean!), but Greg and I stayed up most of the night talking about everything. He is on his way to London tomorrow to find a job and live there for a year, if things work out.

I smelled weed coming from a couple of seats ahead of us. The stewardess didn't say anything to whoever it was, I guess.

I slept about three hours, and when I woke up, I saw the sun rising above the clouds. It was spectacular!

At the Paris airport we stepped into chaos with everyone trying to get through customs. My French still is not that great, so it was weird to hear people speaking it and not be able to understand what they said. I did not have time to stop and listen carefully to try and figure it out. I breathed with relief when a woman from our program helped us get through customs and herded us onto the bus going to our hotel. Greg did not have anyone to meet him, so he got on our bus, too. He is staying at another hotel nearby.

Our Paris hotel is small, but we each have our own room. From my window I can see the Arc de Triomphe and the Paris streets. We were all tired from the long, overnight flight. I collapsed on the bed and slept for a couple of hours.

When I woke up, I took a shower and changed my clothes. I met the other four students on my program. They all seem so much more sophisticated than me and more at ease in France. Barbara is from Connecticut. She took French all through high school and college and has traveled in Europe with her family, so she is fluent in French. Paul is from New Jersey, and he speaks Spanish but not much French. Marianne is from New York City. She speaks some French, more than me. Then there is Edward who is from Louisiana. His family is Creole, I think, and he has been speaking French since he was little. But he says French there is not quite the same as French in France. Anyway, I feel awkward because I only had one semester of French before I came here, and I have never traveled to Europe before, or much of anywhere outside of Michigan.

After we settled into our rooms, we all had lunch at a restaurant nearby. We started with bread and wine, then had crepes, a main dish, salad and fruit. Afterwards, we got on a bus to take a tour of Paris. I actually saw the Eiffel Tower! We climbed to the parapet of Notre Dame (an amazing cathedral) and I stood right next to a gargoyle. He rested his head in his hand and looked like a monkey with folded wings. I took a picture of him.

At dinnertime Greg came to my hotel, and we went out to find a restaurant. We ate at a café, and I stumbled over the French to order for both of us since Greg does not really know French. The waiter spoke to us in English, a bit disdainfully, I thought. We wandered around Paris, past the open markets, and gazed in awe at all the sparkling night lights. Lots of people walked along the streets. They were well-dressed and stylish, and mostly slender. We were in Paris, walking along the Seine and the Left Bank! Notre Dame gleamed in the dark. Like nothing I ever experienced before!

When we went back to Greg's hotel and started climbing the stairs to his room, the woman concierge came out of the downstairs room and yelled at us in French. I think she told us it was forbidden, interdict, but I was not sure what was forbidden. Her husband came out then and told us in English that it was okay. So, we rushed up the stairs, laughing at how weird it all was to be here in Paris.

There was nothing romantic, we just talked. About all kinds of things. He asked me what I thought of existentialism. We had both read The Trial by Kafka. I told him I think we all have to find the meaning in our lives and be true to that. He said he was still looking for that in his life, and that is part of why he came to Europe. I said I want to be the best person I can be and help other people to do that, too. He said he thought I would be a good counselor and told me about Rogerian psychology, which is client-centered.

When it got late, he walked me back to my hotel. I liked him, he was easy to talk to, but I will probably never see him again because he's not going to Nice on our program.

Tomorrow we will take the train to Nice in the south of France. I have only ridden a train once in my life, and it was only to Grand Rapids and back to see the Shrine Circus. I wonder what Nice will be like. It is on the Riviera, the Mediterranean, so I will get to see the sea. I am nervous to be so far from home, not knowing anyone, not speaking French fluently.

But I am excited to be in France. It was my goal since freshman year to study abroad, and thanks to the scholarship I won, I am here!

Mardi, 26 Janvier

Today we left Paris and took the train to Nice. The woman who met us in Paris made sure we got to the train station, gave us our tickets, and we were on our own. I am glad that Barbara is fluent in French, just in case we need to talk to someone.

The train was the kind that had separate compartments. So, the five of us had our own compartment. It was kind of weird because we don't know each other very well. Six hours was time enough for us to start to get to know each other, though. We took turns talking about ourselves, where we come from, what our families are like, what we are studying at University.

When we arrived in Nice, a professor who will teach our classes in sociology, two student liaisons, and a couple of graduate students met us and helped us sort out our luggage. Everyone shook our hands when we were introduced and told us it is the custom when you meet someone. In the States men often shake hands, but women usually don't. I think it's a great custom for everyone to do it. Paul asked about the kiss on both cheeks. We were told that it's more for friends, people you know. And it's usually an "air kiss." One of the student liaisons gave each of us a small amount of money in French francs in case we need money right away. The money is more colorful than in the U.S.

They took us to the old town for dinner. In Old Town we walked down narrow winding cobblestone streets. The buildings smelled old to me, like everything had been sitting here for ages. The streets are so narrow that the buildings seem to loom on either side of them. The restaurant where we ate must have been built centuries ago. The ceiling was low and the room was dimly lit, with candles on the tables. We had a traditional French meal: bread and wine, hors d'oeuvres (tomatoes and sliced potatoes), main dish (I had shrimp), salad (after the meal, not before), dessert (tarts), espresso (strong without milk).

The French people look very stylish. Women wear wool or suede midi skirts with boots and sweaters. Men wear nice pants and shirts, dressier than men in the States. Younger people often have shag haircuts. Lots of people were out "promenading," often with their dogs, and even took their dogs into stores with them. They don't clean up after their dogs, I discovered.

Nice is a very large city, with a population of about 350,000. Much larger than any city I have lived in before. The cars are small, and traffic zips very fast through the narrow streets. There are not many stoplights or stop signs, so I wonder how the cars keep from running into each other. Street signs are often on the side of buildings instead of on separate posts like in the States

The Cité Jean-Medicin where we will stay is on the edge of the city. The complex consists of several dorms, built like modern dorms in the States. It was late by the time we got here. Barbara, Marianne, and I have rooms next to each other on the first floor. Paul and Edward are in the boys' dorm across from our building.

Everything is so different, and so interesting. It is a lot to absorb. I had just enough energy to write this, and now I am going to collapse into bed.

Mercredi, 27 Janvier

Our Cité on the edge of the city is mostly full of international students. On the first floor, a group of women students from Nigeria live in adjacent rooms. They are lively and friendly, and seem to be having a good time. Most of the French students live in a different dorm complex, more in the center of the city and close to the classrooms. I wonder why we are separated from them. Is it because Americans are not good enough to mix with French students, or administrators don't want us to mingle too much and get to know each other?

My room is small, with a twin bed, a nightstand, a desk/dresser with a chair, and shelves in the headboard where I put my transistor radio, a clock and a few books. There is a sink in the room, but the bathrooms are down the hall. The cafeteria serves breakfast and supper, but we will eat dinner (lunch) at the main Cité which we will take a bus to That Cité is where we will have our classes, though, so it makes sense.

I have met students from England, Africa, Thailand, and Latin America. Mostly, everyone is friendly and helpful. Miguel, who grew up in Central America but moved to Chicago when he was eight, speaks Spanish, English, and French fluently. When he is with American students, he is Michael, when he is with French students, he is Michel, and when he is with the Spanish students, they call him Miguel.

When I said how much I wish I had brought my guitar to France, he suggested that when we have a break from classes, he and I join two French students who plan to hitchhike to Spain, and then I can buy a guitar! I have never hitchhiked before, but students here do it all the time. Maybe having a guitar again will make me feel less lonely. I am excited and homesick all at the same time.

Vendredi, 5 Février

I haven't written in my journal for a few days. There are so many things to do to get settled in. I am taking two French classes, one conversational and one more formal French. French spoken in Nice is slightly different from the Parisian French that I learned in my University class. My French is improving, but I still struggle if people talk really fast or use words I don't know. One of my French teachers is patient, but the other one is clearly impatient with my progress, or lack of.

Our professor of sociology lectures twice a week. At least he lectures in English, even though he lives here in France. Sometimes I have a hard time listening to his lectures because I want to be out exploring. There is so much to see and experience.

We are learning about the Tsiganes (gypsies) in France, and it is very interesting. There are 100,000 gypsies in France and two-thirds of them are nomadic. They live in trois groups: Sinti from Italy, who came to France 500 years ago; Gitans from Spain, who also came 500 years ago; and Romani from Central Europe, who came one to two centuries ago. The French government is trying to get them to settle into communities and become acculturated. We are going to visit one of the communities where the government has provided housing and a school.

There are no assignments except for readings and two essays, no exams, and one final paper due by early May. Sounds easy, but some of the readings are in French!

Every day I walk several blocks from our dorm to the Cité in the center of the city where we go to classes. Sometimes I walk with others from our group and sometimes alone. There are a lot of construction workers working on buildings along the street where I usually walk. The men, who I am told are Algerian, sometimes call out to me. I do not understand what they are saying, but I walk faster. This is the fastest route to the main Cité, but maybe I should walk a different way.

The city of Nice is spread along the coast of the Mediterranean. Behind the city are mountains, and you can see houses nestled into the hillside. A wide boulevard, called the Promenade des Anglais runs along the beach with large hotels like the Negresco along one side and a side walk that goes along the beach on the other side.

We often walk along the beach side on our way to class. I am fascinated by the palm trees that line the Promenade, because I have not seen so many before. The trees at home are much different, hardwoods and evergreens.

Lundi, 8 Février

This morning I went to the Prefecture to get my visa so I can stay here as a student for the semester. I was passed from room to room, waiting in between, which seemed very inefficient. At least I understood the French instructions when I had to fill out the forms and when people talked to me.

I got to French class late (not my fault!) and the teacher was not happy about it. I explained why I was late, but that did not seem to help. When I heard a plane passing overhead, I wished I was on it, going home. I thought I wanted to be a traveler, but now I'm not so sure. I miss home, but I want to be an adventurer!

This afternoon I went to the beginner's French to get some extra practice. It was much easier, and I felt more successful. And not so homesick. The teacher was encouraging, and the other students friendly and welcoming.

I thought about what Brian said before I left, that after we finish our senior year in college next year, we should get married. And that sounds very reassuring right now. I know I will get over being homesick, but right now everything seems so different and sometimes confusing.

I went to the Galleries Lafayette and bought a birthday present for Brian and then bought a few groceries at the supermarché, so I have some food to keep in my dorm room. I think of the Riviera as being warm, but it has been pretty cold lately. I hope it will get warmer soon. I did not expect to be wearing a winter coat on the sunny Riviera.

Mardi, 9 Février

When I got to the Cité Université for class, I was surprised to discover that the professors are on strike over their salaries, so we don't have classes today. Edward and I decided to walk along the Mediterranean all the way from the Cité to the top of the Chateau, a hill on one end of the city overlooking the Mediterranean. It was a beautiful blue-sky day. Imagine springtime in February! Sunshine sparkled on the cerulean blue Mediterranean. Lots of people walked along the Promenade or sat in the sun on the beach. Although it is not really a beach to me because a lot of it is covered with small pebbles, not a beautiful sandy beach like we have in Michigan. I stopped to watch a sidewalk artist who was painting the street scene. His picture was full of light and color, and I wished I was a painter and could paint the scenes that I see here.

From the top of the Chateau, we looked out at the city below in three directions and the water in the fourth direction. For a while, I forgot about being homesick because the experience of walking through the old town and the history of everything was so amazing. Narrow streets lined with buildings that were built a long time ago. Very different from the States where even the buildings we think of as old are new compared to Europe.

Edward is easy to talk to. He has that laid back manner of Louisiana (at least as I think of it, because I've never been there). So, I feel relaxed and I can talk about myself and how I am feeling. I think we are a bit attracted to each other, but I don't think I want that or that he does either. Maybe we just feel attracted because it is so nice to have someone with whom we feel comfortable.

In the afternoon we visited a designer clothes factory. They sell clothes to New York City, Texas, and other places. They were preparing for summer and fall fashions. For next winter they were working on sweater-like tops with suede skirts, zippered up the front. We watched how they cut the fabric for the clothing based on the designs they are given, without patterns. I was amazed at how skillful they are.

When we got back to the Cité, I found that I had received four letters from home! Two from Brian. He misses me! How I miss him! One from my best friend from high school and one from my mom. I think she is worried about me because she has to wait for my letters to arrive to know how I am doing. It is weird not to be able to call home, but to make an international call we have to go to the post office and wait in line, and phone calls are very expensive. When I was at college at home, I usually called home from the phone at the end of the hall once a week to please my mom. Now I can't call anyone. Feels weird!

Mercredi, 10 Février

An interesting day! While I sat on a bench at the beach watching the waves of the Mediterranean roll into shore, an Algerian boy sat down next to me and said, "Bonjour." He looked about the same age as me. I was surprised and not sure how I felt about a stranger sitting beside me like that, but he introduced himself and so I told him my name. He said, "Ah, American." And smiled. He seemed harmless.

He didn't speak English and my French is still not fluent, but we were able to communicate about ourselves and why we are in France. He told me he is from Constantine and is here with his brothers and uncles who work on the construction projects. I hope they are not the ones who whistle and call out to me when I go by! I am not sure what they are saying, but it makes me uncomfortable. Anyway, my Algerian (that's how I think of him) is not currently working, so he seems a bit lost. He told me he does not go into the French cafés because Algerians are not welcome there. He always walks to the Algerian section of town to have a coffee. He taught me a few phrases in Arabic. This is probably not how they are spelled, but how they sounded to me:

Saba el rire – bonjour
Emce el rire – bonsoir
Quie fair usmic – What is your name?

He took me to where he lives with his uncle, brothers, and some other Algerians. It is in a shabby, one-story building, just one big room full of cots, a table with chairs in one corner, and a cupboard with a hotplate and some dishes along one wall. He showed me pictures of his home and family in Algeria, and told me how much he misses them. I understood his homesickness!

Afterwards, I thought maybe it was not a good idea for me to go there with him by myself, but it felt okay and I was not worried. He is very gentle. Lonely, I think, because all the other men he lives with are at work every day.

I remember that one of the French students who helps us adjust to our stay in France lived with her family in Algeria. I will have to ask her more about it. I know it was a French colony for a while, but there was a revolution and the French had to leave. There seem to be a lot of Algerians working here, but they are not really accepted as part of France.

This evening we went to a French comedy, Le Distrait. It was only in French without English subtitles, so I did not understand everything. But there was a lot of action comedy, so I was able to follow a lot of it. Made me feel like I am fitting in, being a bit French.

Yawning, Tara closes the journal. She will continue reading it tomorrow. She leans back against the pillow and imagines her aunt traveling to Europe on her own at age 20, not knowing anyone. France sounds so exciting when her aunt writes about it. Although her aunt was homesick, she seemed to meet people and make friends.

The first time Tara went to Europe, she went with her high school Spanish class. All the arrangements were made for her, and she went with one of her best friends. Later, when she was in college, she and her roommate spent a month in London at a writing workshop. It all seemed so easy.

Interesting that the professors at the U in Nice were on strike, and the students did not seem to think that was unusual. Tara does not remember her professors ever going on strike while she was at the U.

Tara has never thought about gypsies. In stories and sometimes TV shows, they are often presented as people who are exotic, as thieves or fortune tellers.

It surprises her that Aunt Becca walked off with an Algerian whom she'd just met to the place where he lived. Would Tara have done that if she had met him? She does not think so. Maybe there are too many scary things happening to women these days, and women are more cautious about safety. Or, maybe she would have been just as nonchalant about it at age 20. Her aunt was able to accept this young Algerian man as a friend, even though she felt uneasy about the Algerian men who called out to her from the construction sites.

Five

Summer 2023

Maria peers around the edge of the window trying not to be seen and watches the path that goes to the bluff of Lake Michigan. It is hard being stuck inside this farmhouse, but she does not want to meet people who are hiking on the trail. No one comes or goes from the bluff, and it looks quiet. She opens the back door a crack and checks to see if anyone is around.

Cautiously, she walks around to the front of the house, down the hill to the trail across the field. Walking quickly and listening for any sound of voices, she reaches the bluff and looks out over the water. Far out in the lake, gusts of wind churn up waves that rush onto shore with a swooshing sound. She imagines what it would be like if her life were just ordinary and she could come here with her family, feeling no fear.

Back at the farmhouse, she rations out the food and water she has brought with her. Earlier today when she packed it, she did not realize how hungry and thirsty she might get in a day. She does not have enough to last very long. She eats slowly, telling herself she is full.

Then she calls her mom as she does every evening when her mom gets home from work. As the phone rings, she takes a deep breath. She can't cry. She has to sound like she is okay.

"Hello, Maria. How are you? I am so worried since Grandma had a stroke."

"No worries, Mama. I am staying with Grandma's neighbors for now. Lorena and Manuel are busy tonight, but Lorena says she will call you tomorrow to let you know all is okay."

"That is very kind of them. They will take good care of you. Here is your sister. She is eager to talk to you."

Maria finishes the conversation as quickly as she can so she will not let on how sad and lonely she is and promises to call again tomorrow. After she disconnects the call, she wipes tears from her eyes. She lied to her mom, something she never does, but she could not tell her she was here in this farmhouse, all alone. Her mother is far away and could not help her.

She drags the only rocking chair over to the window, pulls her book out of her backpack, and tries to read while there is still enough light to see the page. Why had not she considered that there would be no lamps, no electricity?

As the sun goes down, darkness closes in. A couple of stars peek through the clouds, but it is a moonless night. Maria shivers, zips up her sweatshirt, and pulls the hood over her head. A wild cry resounds in the night air, and something scratches and snuffles outside the house.

Coming out here to get away seemed like a good idea earlier today. Before it got dark, when it seemed no one was around. Now, she isn't so sure. Can she really stay in this old farmhouse? She had not thought about the lack of furniture, the lack of a bed with sheets and blankets.

She sobs with all the feelings of grief she has been holding inside. If she were a wolf, she would start to howl. She wants her mom and her sister. She wants her grandma to be well, to be herself. She wants to go back to Ann Arbor where her friends are. She does not want to be here.

Exhausted, she slumps in the chair. There is nothing she can do tonight. She made sure the doors and windows were locked. The window in the back door is cracked where earlier today she forced the door open. Luckily, the lock was old and did not hold very well. She has pulled the table over in front of the door. No one can get in without her hearing them, she tells herself. She will sleep upstairs and pull the old dresser in front of the bedroom door. Maybe she can walk back into town to buy a few things that she needs with the small amount of money she bought with her.

Things will look better in the morning, when it is daylight again. She will figure out what to do then.

Six

Tara looks around the basement. It is mostly neat and tidy with an exercise bike and a rowing machine on a rug in one corner, two groups of boxes stored neatly along one wall with a space between them, and miscellaneous items sitting on shelves.

"Where do we start?"

"Let's start with those boxes. Some of them have been there since we moved in, I think. Time to clean things out, get rid of what's not needed."

Tara hates sorting out people's basements, but somehow sorting helps Uncle Robb cope with the loss of her aunt. She starts to open one of the boxes.

"No, not those. That's Becca's stuff. The ones on the left are mine, probably nothing I still need." He gestures to the left side.

There are boxes of clothes that Uncle Robb has not worn for a few years and boxes of textbooks from his college days. The next one she opens is more interesting.

"Is this yours from when you were a child?" She pulls out an engine from an electric train set.

Uncle Robb smiles. "My electric train set. I'd forgotten it was down here. My dad and I set it up in our basement and built a whole town for it."

"Why didn't we get it out when I came to visit?"

Rob shakes his head. "I guess it didn't occur to me that a little girl would like a train set. But, of course, that was ridiculous." He grimaces. "Sexist maybe?"

"No doubt. Glad times have changed about things like that. What do you want to do with it?"

"Leave it. Maybe we could get it out again sometime and set it up. See if it works."

Tara smiles. "That's a great idea." She closes the box and opens another. This one contains some old dishes and pots and pans. Probably no longer needed.

She looks over at Uncle Robb, who is gazing at a photograph. "What did you find?"

He hands it to her, a picture of four teenage boys posing with instruments in a nonchalant stance, doing their best to look cool. The drum set has a name on the bass drum, "The Rogues." She looks closely at one of the guitar players. "Is that you?"

Uncle Robb laughs. "Afraid so. We look pretty cool, huh?"

"Actually, you do. When was this? I didn't know you played the guitar in a band. Did you play lead guitar?"

"No, rhythm. We had a band in high school for a couple of years, played at various small-town gigs. We even had an agent for a few months, planned to make the big time."

"I wish I could have seen you play. Look at that hair, sort of a Beatles style, I'd say. We should definitely save this."

Uncle Robb smiles. "Good memories."

At the end of the day, Uncle Robb takes a nap while she showers and catches up on text messages. Several of her friends have texted condolences about her aunt, saying they miss her and asking when she is coming back.

In the evening, she and Uncle Robb sit on the back porch. The air feels warm and gentle in the soft darkness. An owl hoots in the distance.

"Sounds like a barred owl." Uncle Robb listens. Another hoot in answer to the first one. "There goes another one. Probably a conversation about getting together later. That time of year for owls."

"Huh. I don't think I've heard an owl like that before." Tara listens to the conversation back and forth. "So, what happened after you and Aunt Becca went to the café? When did the two of you start seeing each other?"

"As I said, I was dating someone else. But I never stopped thinking about Rebecca. There was just something about her."

"You didn't stay with that person you were dating?"

"No, we liked each other, but we both moved on. Then the next year I was walking on campus at the U of M, and there was Becca, coming across the Quad. I remembered her right away. I stopped and just then she looked up. She had a slight frown on her face, as if she were trying to remember me.

"'Have we met?' she said, and then she smiled. 'Yes, you stopped when I was sitting on the porch being sad. Robb, isn't it?'

"I smiled back and said, yes, I was. I was thrilled that she remembered my name. I asked her how she was, what she was doing these days."

"We started walking together and she told me she was back at the U getting her MA in social work. I told her I was doing some research for a former professor.

"Your aunt said her teaching degree hadn't helped her to get a job. There didn't seem to be many openings for a woman to teach social studies, because most job listings included coaching men's sports with a position teaching those subjects. Two of her roommates had teaching degrees but couldn't get jobs. One was going back to school for a master's degree to become a school psychologist, and one was going home to work in her father's hardware store.

"The only one of them with a real job was the one who was an artist, but got a degree in biology and landed a job in a lab at a pharmaceutical company. So, Becca decided to get a social work degree and see if she could help people.

"I told her it was the same with my roommates. One with a history degree was going back to his summer job and would keep applying for better jobs. Another was going to work at his dad's construction company. I was embarrassed that I didn't have a concrete plan, but she understood.

"She had to get to a class, so we exchanged phone numbers. And that was the start of something special. We started out as friends, and then it moved beyond that."

"So, you became friends and then lovers. And stayed that way all these years. Two of the lucky ones." Tara sighs.

Uncle Robb rocks his chair slowly, back and forth, staring into the velvet darkness.

"I found a box of stones in a shoebox on a shelf in the kitchen. Where did they come from? What are they for?"

"That's Becca's collection. Every time we walk on the beach, she finds an interesting shell or stone. She is…" Uncle Robb stops, starts over. "She was fascinated by the different kinds of minerals in the rocks, different colors, you know. And fossils that were dropped when the glacier melted. She loved fossils. I called her the Beach Magpie." Uncle Robb looks forlorn. "I guess she won't find them anymore."

Tara reaches out and pats his arm. "Do you mind if I take them? I was thinking I would hike some of her favorite trails and make small cairns in her memory."

"She would like that."

"I felt terrible when I couldn't come to Aunt Becca's memorial service. All during the pandemic, I didn't get Covid. And then at the worst time, I came down with it and had to stay home. I felt so bad that I wasn't here for you." Tara blinks back the tears in her eyes.

Uncle Robb pats her shoulder. "It couldn't be helped. I knew you were here in spirit. And there were so many people at the memorial who had fond memories of Becca."

"She knew a lot of people and was always willing to help someone when they needed it."

"Maybe making the cairns will give you a chance to say your own goodbye. She would be pleased by that."

Soon her uncle says good night and goes into the house. Tara watches the stars begin to twinkle in the inky sky and then goes to her room.

She opens her laptop to check her email. Some suspicious invitations to accept millions of dollars from an unknown relative. A few solicitations from organizations. One from Planned Parenthood reassures her that abortion is legal in Michigan and she has a right to get an abortion.

Abortion rights are complicated since the Supreme Court overturned Roe v Wade. Now some states protect women's right to make their own decisions, and some forbid them from deciding for themselves. What would it be like to live in a state where they wouldn't let you get an abortion even in cases of rape or incest, or if the child wasn't going to be able to breathe on its own? How would it feel to know that the laws took away your right to choose for yourself about your own body?

She checks the news feed that she reads every day. Fierce fighting in Ukraine, more people dying and cities damaged. A discussion regarding Ukraine's path to join NATO. A Russian soldier surrendering to a Ukrainian drone. She wishes Russia had not invaded Ukraine, that Ukrainians would be allowed to live peacefully.

She closes the laptop and takes out the journal.

Seven

Nice, France
1971

Vendredi, 12 Février

This morning I went to the cafeteria for breakfast. There were only a few students eating, no one I knew. While I ate bread and jam and drank café au lait, I watched the people at the counter cutting baguettes. They have a special machine that is like a tube. The baguettes are stuck in lengthwise, the machine is turned on, and evenly cut chunks come out of the bottom. I thought it was a pretty cool machine, designed just for French bread.

Today after classes we visited the Russian Church that was built by Tsar Nicolas II of Russia for the Russian elite who vacationed in Nice. After the Revolution of 1917 many White Russians settled in Nice. The church is beautiful and colorful, with several striped domes around the top of it.

Then we ate ice cream at Le Negresco, a very fancy hotel and restaurant that looks kind of like a small castle with a pink dome on top and gold letters that spell out the name. The inside is decorated in a very grand style. I don't think I could afford to eat there except for the ice cream.

In the evening Miguel came to my room. I was surprised to see him as he hadn't done that before. We just talked for a while, and he told me about how he always wanted to be a bullfighter. I could not imagine how anyone would want to do that! You would have to kill the poor bull in the end. But Miguel said it was a noble profession and much respected in Spain. He compared it to hunting in the States, and said that it is more noble to confront your opponent (the bull) than to shoot it when it can't see you. I think maybe neither is necessarily noble, but I did not argue with him.

We also discussed what we think freedom means. We compared the freedom of the individual with the freedom of the group and agreed that we are both in favor of freedom for all. Then he told me funny stories about the howler monkeys who lived near his house in Latin America, and made me laugh.

Samedi, 13 Février

In the States today was Valentine's Day. In Nice we celebrated
Carnival, like Mardi Gras in New Orleans, I think. Three of
us went to watch the parade at Place Masséna. The floats were
fantastic, and people threw fistfuls of confetti. So much confetti rained down on us that we moved to the edge of the
crowd to get away from it. One of the floats had a large figure
wearing what looked like a Native American headdress riding
a horse with several weird, colorful figures around it. I'm not
sure what it represented or what it had to do with Carnival.

I have been in Nice for three weeks now. It's Saturday and
I am thinking about what I would be doing over the weekend
if I were back in the States. Probably I would do some studying, and Brian and I would go out with friends tonight. It
would be great to just speak English and not feel like I was
struggling so much to understand and be understood!

The five of us who are on our program stick together a lot,
and we usually speak English, but I should be braver and at-
tempt to speak to people in French more often. What made
me think I could come all the way to France by myself and
make this work? I've never really been anywhere, and everyone else seems so much more experienced.

This evening we all went to the cinema to see Little Big
Man, along with a couple of French students that Miguel
knows. I read the book for my American Lit class last semester. The movie was in English, but there were French subtitles. It was fun to see how the English was translated into
French. Like the book, the movie made me think more about
what it was like for Native Americans to have people take
away their land and try to drive them out of places where
their ancestors had lived for a long time.

Afterward, we all went to a café. One of the French students told me that the French are very interested in the "wild

west of cowboys and Indians" because they have never had that kind of time in their history. I said that in the States, we use the term Native American instead of Indian.

I told them about the book Bury My Heart at Wounded Knee that came out last year and how lots of people read it and realized that Native Americans had been massacred by the army so that white people could take their land. How in the Battle of Wounded Knee, nearly 300 Lakota people were shot and killed, including women and children. The American Indian Movement organized to improve the lives of Native Americans, who are still not treated very well in the States. The French students taught me "L'Internationale," a sort of universal freedom anthem.

Vendredi, 19 Février

I was excited this morning when I woke up. Miguel and I started off on our big adventure hitchhiking to Spain today! We met at the bus stop near the Cité and took a bus to the edge of the city. Then we stood by the road and tried to get rides. Since I haven't hitchhiked before, I had no idea what to expect. At first it was easy, because one of the professors that Miguel knows stopped right away and gave us a ride all the way to Aix-en-Provence. He asked me questions about the States and what I thought of France.

Outside Aix, a couple in a deux chevaux (that's a "two-horse" car) picked us up after we waited about half an hour and gave us a ride to Narbonne. They had some fruit and bread and cheese that they shared with us. By the time they dropped us off, it was evening.

We waited four hours in Narbonne for a ride, and we stamped our feet to warm them up after standing outside for so long. There was not much traffic so we walked up and down, trying to keep warm. Miguel smokes Gauloises, like lots of students here do. I have never smoked before, but I was so bored standing in the cold waiting that I tried one. It was pretty strong, but I kind of liked it. Finally, we decided to take the train to Montpelier.

Samedi, 20 Février

We got into Montpelier this morning, and we did not have to wait very long before a kind woman picked us up and drove us all the way to the Spanish border. We hiked over the Pyrenees into Spain. Near the Mediterranean where we crossed the mountains, the Pyrenees are large, gray, and craggy with lots of green trees, but not as steep as they would be farther west. I thought they were very striking. When we crossed the border from France into Spain, Miguel had tears in his eyes because he was so happy to be in Spain. It reminded him of his childhood before his family moved to Chicago.

When we arrived in Barcelona, we went to the small hotel where the two French girls were staying. It was the first time I had met them, and they were very nice. Michelle spoke some English so we were able to communicate right away. Her friend Hélène spoke French and Spanish, so we did not talk as much, but she and Miguel enjoyed some Spanish conversation. They were both excited about being in Spain and speaking Spanish.

Michelle and Hélène took us to a restaurant that they knew from a previous visit. I had salad, Spanish bread, fried shrimp and flan. It was delicious! And we all talked and laughed a lot, especially because we could not always understand each other.

There were no rooms at their hotel, but they told us about another hotel a few blocks away, so we went there and got a room together for $2.00. I was not sure about sharing a room, because I don't know Miguel that well, but the price was right and I figured it would be okay. What would I do if Miguel wanted to sleep in the same bed? I feel close to him and am starting to feel attracted to him. Fortunately, he just tucked me in and kissed my forehead.

Dimanche, 21 Février

In the morning after breakfast, we met the French girls at a cathedral. They had already made friends with three Spanish students. We did folk dancing in front of the cathedral, and then the Spanish students invited us to a party at their apartment that night.

At the party, people took turns playing guitars and we all sang. We drank some Spanish wine, and the Spanish students made us all laugh with their impersonations of the fascists who control Spain. They said they would not do something like that in public because they could be arrested by the fascist guards. We have seen the Guardia Civil (civil guards) on the street corners, wearing their shiny patent leather hats and carrying rifles (some kind of long gun, I don't know what they are). They make me nervous, but so far, they haven't bothered us. When it was quite late, we all went to a café for dinner. The Spanish seem to eat dinner around 10:00 pm. On the way back to the hotel, we sang and sort of danced down the street.

Lundi, 22 Février

On our last day in Barcelona, one of the Spanish students took us to a music store where we could try out guitars. I picked out a guitar and a case for it. I am très content to finally have a guitar to play while I am in France

In the afternoon we walked to the cathedral of the sacred family. On our way there, we saw a short demonstration in the street but did not know what people were demonstrating about. The cathedral is not finished, and I think it is kind of ugly as it is. On our way back to our hotel, we stopped and ate helados fraise (strawberry ice cream). I thought it tasted better than French ice cream. I like Barcelona.

Mercredi, 24 Février

Yesterday we started hitchhiking back to France. I had to carry my guitar all the way back to Nice, and that was not so easy. Especially when we walked into the wind through the Pyrenees Mountains between Spain and France.

We got a ride with a truck driver who drove very fast through the mountains with no guardrail on the edge of the road. He shared his sardine sandwiches and a thermos of wine with us. He insisted I drink a bit of wine to warm me up because I was really cold from standing outside waiting for rides. And the wine did warm me up. On another ride I sat in the back with the man's dog. I miss my dog at home, and this one was a Brittany spaniel just like mine at home!

In Narbonne we were picked up by a couple of students. They fed us and gave us tickets to eat at the Resto U in Montpellier. Students have been so kind to us on our travels! Out last ride set us down in the cold and dark with little traffic, still 70 kilometers from Nice. We finally got a ride to Fréjus and decided to take a train, but it was the middle of the night when we arrived, and the train station was closed. We had to sit in the cold and wait for it to open. We didn't have enough money for tickets, so we got passes to pay when we arrived in Nice. I was so tired by the time we got here!

I was sad to say goodbye to Miguel as I have grown really fond of him, and he took good care of me on this trip. I know I will see him often, but it won't be the same.

Jeudi, 25 Février

In French class today each of us had to tell in French what we did during the school break. I was able to relate the whole story to the class in French. I was really proud, and the teacher seemed pleased at my progress.

Miguel came to find me at the Cité at lunchtime. He sat close to me and held my hand when he walked me to class after lunch. He pulled me into a doorway and kissed me! I think we are starting something, but neither of us said anything. For one thing, it seems like we will never be alone. There are always other students around, and men and women are not allowed in each other's rooms in the dorm after 5:00. I think we are both shy about letting other people know we are attracted to each other, but I am sure they have guessed.

Should I say something? Will he? And what am I doing? When I left Brian at home, I was definitely not planning on getting into a relationship while I was here. Would that be a big mistake? Probably!!! It seems like a lot of foreign students here are getting involved with someone. I am not sure what to do. And having sex with someone seems much freer here than it did at home.

Samedi, 27 Février

I got to sleep in this morning because it's Saturday. This after-noon we went on a field trip to Arènes Cimiez where the old Roman city of Cemenelum was located. It was the Roman capital of the Riviera for 400 years! The only parts of it you can see are ruins of the arena and the baths, mostly crumbling walls and columns, but you can still see where a door and a window have been. Nearby is a monastery, a cemetery where some famous people like Matisse are buried, and the Musée Matisse. The Musée has many of his work and his possessions. I liked the paintings he did for the chapel and his drawings. He had a good sense of anatomy.

Had dinner with Edward and a student who is from the West Indies. A guy from the Canary Islands and one from Syria also joined us. I love meeting people from all over the world!

Miguel and I went with a couple of French students and a couple of students from Latin America to see an old movie about the Spanish Civil War in the 1930s. I had not learned anything about this civil war before. The Spanish Republicans were very brave to fight the fascist Nationalists. Maybe World War II would not have happened if the fascists had been soundly defeated in Spain! What did the U.S. think about all this? I have studied WWII but never heard anything about what happened in Spain. Weird.

Many of the students here are very interested in politics. After the movie, we went to a café with some of the French students. They asked me about the involvement of the U.S. in the Vietnam War, and they are clear that they don't think the U.S. should be there. The French were there before the U.S., and the students did not like that either. Of course, I agreed with them and told them about the antiwar movement in the States.

I told them about the draft lottery. How the women in my dorm went down to the lounge to watch the drawing of birthdates that would determine the order in which young men would be called up to serve in the military. Those whose boyfriends and relatives got high numbers and would not be called up soon cheered or gave a sigh of relief. Some of those of us whose boyfriends were given low numbers cried. Others like me started thinking about emigrating to Canada or how our boyfriends might get medical deferments. We had heard that there are doctors who are sympathetic to draft resisters and might be willing to diagnose exemptions.

Miguel and the other students told me about the French student rebellion in May 1968. There were demonstrations and general strikes, and the occupation of some universities. They were rebelling against perceived injustices by governments — including the Johnson administration in the States — and were opposed to the draft and the United States' involvement in the Vietnam War. Workers from some of the plants joined the protest movement, and 10 million workers went on strike. Factories closed or were occupied by workers. There was no gasoline, no trains, no mail delivery. Economic life in France ground to a halt.

The students were also protesting what they felt was a patriarchal system with strict rules in the family and at the schools. They wanted their personal freedom. One of the French students, Françoise, said they envied the freedom American students seemed to have, especially women, because the feminist movement was more advanced in the States than it is here.

Miguel seems to know everybody and everyone likes him. When he is around, the world seems brighter, more fun.

Got a box of chocolate chip cookies from my roommates back in the States. Tasted just like home. They sent a letter in which each of them said what classes they are taking, what they are doing. Patty met someone new whom she started dating. Hope that goes well for her. I miss all the discussions we shared last semester. But studying in Europe was something I really wanted to do, and I am excited to be here.

Tara thinks about what she has read. Her aunt was learning many things that were new to her. Some of the French students sound very political, and there were often political discussions. Different issues than today, but a lot the same, too.

She is impressed that her aunt knew about the struggles of Indigenous people. Back then, Tara had thought, most people did not really understand what had happened. Cowboy and Indian shows on TV made the Indians into fearsome warriors, not real people. These days Indigenous people speak up and make their presence known, especially around protecting the environment and reclaiming their homelands. The Secretary of the Interior is an Indigenous woman.

Tara is curious about the French student rebellion in 1968. It sounds like it was a big deal, and thousands of students were involved, as well as working people.

The fact that there used to be a draft and all eighteen-year-old boys/men had to register for it surprised her. How weird that would be. Her generation just takes for granted that the army is volunteer, although some kids join up because they don't see better options.

She also could not imagine traveling around Spain with fascist guards carrying rifles standing on street corners. When she went to Spain with her Spanish class, Spain was not like that.

Tara laughs when she thinks about her aunt smoking cigarettes. Did her aunt continue smoking while she was in France? Aunt Becca always told Tara that smoking is bad for you. Tara never told her aunt about the time when she was fifteen and had a crush on this guy, so started hanging out with him and his friends who smoked behind the school after hours. She smoked cigarettes for a few weeks, and eventually her mom smelled the smoke and she quit. Tara wonders why she did not tell her aunt. Maybe she did not want to disappoint her.

From the pages of the journal, it was becoming more apparent that her aunt was in a relationship with Miguel, something Tara was very curious about. It must have been a big conflict for her when she was still technically in a relationship with Brian at home.

Her phone pings. It's her mom. Tara feels guilty that she hasn't texted her mom for a few days. She picks up the phone and calls her.

"Hi, Mom. Sorry I didn't text."

"Hi, hon. How's everything going? Are you feeling settled in there? How's Uncle Robb doing? He and Becca were so close."

"I'm doing OK. Robb is sad but doing better all the time. How about you?" Tara knows that her mom must be feeling as bereft about losing her sister as she herself is about losing her aunt.

"I think about my sister Becca a lot. We did not always agree about things, but she was always there for me when I needed her. I always thought she would outlive me, that she would always be here."

"She was always there for me, too. I'm sorry she is not here now for you."

"It's a lot to take in. Anyway, we miss you. Take care of yourself."

"I will. You, too. I'll call you soon."

Eight

Summer 2023

Tara decides to walk the Farm Trail again to build a stone cairn in her aunt's memory, a way to say goodbye.

She lets Taffy out of the car and heads down the trail. Taffy trots in front of her, tail bobbing, nose sniffing the air. When she is a short way ahead, she stops and waits for Tara to catch up.

Tara breathes in the crisp, fresh air as the brisk summer wind riffles her hair. She climbs steadily up the sloping trail. When it levels out, she stands at the top and looks in all directions. The trees spread a canopy of deep green throughout the woods. When Tara gets to the old farm buildings, Taffy races up the hill toward the farmhouse.

"Come, Taffy. Not today. We explored that last time."

Taffy stops, barks twice, and looks at Tara.

"Come on. You can run across the field." She follows the narrow path to the left, through the field of tall grasses that make her feel like she is crossing a prairie. Taffy barks again, bounds down the hill, and catches up to her.

Tara pushes carefully through a patch of raspberry bushes that are beginning to stretch their prickly branches into the path. Too soon to enjoy their berries. She remembers hiking with her aunt in August, stopping to pick raspberries along the trail. She ate so many that she finally had to stop.

Through the trees she glimpses splashes of blue. At the end of the trail, she again stands on the bluff and looks out at the vast lake. Small whitecaps crest the waves that swoosh into the shore. In a protected spot near the edge of the bluff, she builds a small rock cairn. This one includes a couple of fossils of plant life from long ago.

"In memory of Aunt Becca who loved the natural world and taught me how to identify plants and flowers and the calls of many birds. Thank you. I will always remember." She sits on a rock and watches mist rising from the water far out on the horizon.

Walking back through the field, she spots a couple of deer on the far side near the thick stand of trees. She snaps on Taffy's leash. Her dog has not chased deer in the past, but Tara is not sure if she would or not.

Back at the barn, Taffy barks and tugs on the leash, pulling Tara toward the hill that leads to the farmhouse. Tara frowns.

"What is it with you today?" She unhooks the leash. "Fine. Go."

Taffy dashes partway up the hill, turns and looks at Tara, then dashes the rest of the way up to the house. She waits for Tara to follow her to the top of the hill. Taffy races to the back of the house and paws at the back door.

"You really want to get in there, but I'm sure the door is locked."

Suddenly, she hears a clattering sound and then a thump. She steps back. Is there someone in there? She hears a moan and a sob. Someone is inside.

"What do you think it is, Taffy?" Taffy looks up at her. She listens again. Another moaning sound. Maybe a voice, faint, distressed.

"What should I do?" A quiet sob.

Tara turns the doorknob. The door is not locked, and she pushes it open and steps inside. Taffy crowds in behind her.

"Hello. Anyone need help?"

And then there is silence.

"Come on, Taffy, I think we have to check it out. Stay with me."

Tara and Taffy walk slowly through the kitchen and into the parlor. Lying at the foot of the stairs, Tara sees a slim figure with long, dark, curly hair, a young girl.

Tara calls out softly. "Hi, my name is Tara and I am here with my dog, Taffy. We would like to help you. We won't hurt you. I promise. And Taffy loves meeting new people."

A faint voice. "Okay."

Tara sees that the girl is probably a young teenager. Her leg is twisted to one side. Maybe she has hurt her ankle. Tara looks around for another person. What is this girl doing here by herself? She does not look old enough to have driven herself here.

The girl looks up with teary, brown eyes. Then glances with interest at Taffy.

"Did you hurt your ankle? May I look at it?"

The girl nods. Taffy lies down near her.

"May I pet the dog?"

"She would like that. Her name is Taffy."

"Like the candy?"

Tara laughs. "Yes, she is very sweet."

The girl reaches out and gently strokes Taffy's head and ears. "She's really soft."

Tara kneels beside the girl, gently touches the ankle. It does not seem swollen. "My name is Tara," she says again.

"I'm Maria."

"Pretty name. Do you want to try to stand on your foot?"

"Is it broken?"

"I don't think so. Can you move it?"

Maria swivels her foot back and forth, her eyes shut, her mouth clenched. "It hurts."

"Here, I will help you up and we'll see if you can put any weight on it."

Maria nods. Tara stands and holds out her arms. Maria grips them and Tara pulls her up. Maria stands on one foot and Tara helps her to balance.

"Try putting your foot down."

Maria tentatively puts her foot down but pulls it up again. "It hurts, but I think I could limp a little on it." She takes a couple of halting steps.

"Do you hurt anywhere else?"

"I think I landed on my arm."

"Can you move it?"

"Sort of, but it hurts."

"Did you hit your head?"

"No, I protected it with my arm."

"Is anyone with you? Someone I should try to find?"

Maria shakes her head quickly from side to side.

"Do you live nearby?"

Maria shakes her head again. "Thanks for your help. I'm fine now. I should get going."

"Going where?" What was Maria doing out here? "Did someone drop you off? Are they coming back soon?"

"Yes, yes, they will be here very soon."

"Do you have your phone with you?" Why hadn't Maria called someone to come and help her?

Maria shakes her head. "I must have left it in the car."

"I can call them so they could come and get you. I will help you back to the entrance and wait with you until they come."

"No need. I am fine. You can continue your hike."

"I can't just leave you here. Are you in trouble of some kind? Are you hiding from someone?"

"No, no, all is okay."

"Have you been staying at the house?" Tara remembered when she and Taffy had walked around the house and Taffy seemed to think there was something, or someone, there.

Maria looks frightened.

"Don't' worry. I won't tell anyone. How long have you been by yourself? What do you have to eat?"

"A couple of days. I brought what we had at our house. I eat just a little of it each day so it will last."

"No one knows you are here?"

"I don't think so. I watch out the window and when I see hikers, I stay out of the way. People don't usually come here at night, so I go outside just before it gets dark. It gets very dark inside at night." Maria shivers.

"That all sounds very hard. When we came here last time, Taffy seemed to sense someone was in the house. And today she insisted we come back here."

"Dogs are really smart." Maria strokes Taffy's back. Taffy wags her tail. "She saw me when you walked by earlier. I hurried into the house, but she knew I was here."

"I see. She tried to tell me that she saw you, I guess. Isn't there someone who will be worried about you?"

"Just my grandma."

"Where is your grandma?"

"She usually works during the days and I am on my own. But she had a stroke and is in the hospital, and she was worried about me being alone. I don't want to go into care. I have heard kids at school talk about it. So, I left."

"You don't know if your grandma is well then. Perhaps she is ready to go home. She will be worried about you."

"I know. I did not know what to do."

"Come with me. We will find out how your grandma is and if she is still in the hospital. You could stay with Taffy and me for a while, with your grandma's permission."

"Really?"

"You don't know me very well, but you can't stay here by yourself. I live with my uncle. You will like him, and you will be safe with us." She has not asked her uncle how he feels about it, and she needs to call him. Is she doing the right thing? She does not know this girl, or anything about her. Still, she cannot leave Maria here on her own. If things don't work out, she will have to find other arrangements.

"You have things here that we should take with us?"

"Just a few things."

Tara takes that as a sign that Maria accepts her suggestion to leave with her.

"We'll take it slowly. We can stop and rest whenever you need to."

The kitchen is sparsely furnished. Maria's food is neatly organized on the table. There is not much left, two granola bars and an apple. There is no working refrigerator, so Maria must have eaten anything perishable right away. What would Maria have done in the next day or so when the food was gone? A water bottle sits next to the food. How did Maria get enough water? Tara finds a plastic bag lying on the counter and stashes the food in it.

In the front room is a wooden rocking chair that looks like it has been there for a long time. A sleeping bag and pillow lie on the floor next to a small backpack.

"Come and sit in the rocker and rest your foot. I'll pack everything up and carry it for you back to the car." She expects Maria to protest, but she slumps with exhaustion into the chair, rocking back and forth and looking out the window. It does not take long to pack things up, and then Tara hefts the pack onto her back. Taffy paces around the room, back and forth between Tara and Maria.

"Ready?" Tara smiles. Maria nods. Tara helps her to stand up and they start the slow trek back to the car. Maria holds

Tara's arm and does her best to limp along beside her. Taffy walks closely by her side and Maria reaches down to pet her every now and then. It's slow-going. Tara distracts her by pointing out the flowers and trees they see, explaining about Sleeping Bear Dunes, the Indigenous people who lived here since long ago, and the people who settled in the area to farm.

Tara helps Maria into the front seat and lets Taffy into the back. While she stows Maria's pack in the trunk, she calls Uncle Robb.

Nine

He answers on the third ring. "Tara? Everything okay?"

"Fine. Well, sort of." She gives him a quick version about finding Maria, Maria's fear of being sent away, and her plan to give her a temporary place to stay. He does not answer for a few seconds.

"Uncle Robb, if you don't like the idea, you should say. It's your house."

"No, you're right to help her out. We can't let her be on her own like that."

"Thanks. I did not know what else to do with her."

Tara is quiet as she drives back toward town, letting Maria adjust to the changes ahead. Suddenly, Maria begins to talk.

"Mi madre y mi hermana were deported in May because they are not citizens, and they were here illegally. I was born here, so I am a citizen of this country. Mi madre wanted me to stay here with mi abuela because it is safer for me here than it would be for me where my mother lives. And I could go to school and get a good education. Maybe go to college."

Maria sniffles, trying not to cry.

"So, I stayed with a friend's family to finish out the school year, and then I moved up here to live with my grandma. But I am so lonely without the rest of my family. I want to go and live with my mother and sister again."

She wipes her eyes with the back of her hand. Tara pulls a clean tissue out of her pocket and hands it to her.

"At first, I stayed at the hospital when my grandma had a stroke. I was afraid that she would die, and I would be all alone. She recovered a little, and I was so relieved. But she was partly paralyzed on one side. She cannot talk very well and does not remember things sometimes. The hospital said she needs to go to a rehab center where people would do therapy to help her recover. They do not know how long it will take.

"My grandma wrote a note to the nurse asking her to call a friend so the friend would find someone to take care of me. I was scared that the hospital people knew I was alone, and I would have to go live with someone else. Someone I did not even know. So, I left the hospital before someone could arrive to take me away."

"Your grandmother does not know you are here?"

Maria shakes her head. "I could not tell her. She would be worried."

Tara thinks that is an understatement. She hesitates to say anything. What will Maria's grandmother say about what Maria has done? About Tara taking her home with her?

"That would be very distressing. What made you go to the old farm and stay in the farmhouse?"

"My grandma's neighbors brought us here once to show us the old farm and the view of Lake Michigan. I saw the farmhouse where people used to live. I thought I could stay there until my grandma is well and can go home and no one would find me."

"How did you get all the way out here from the hospital?"

Maria hesitates. "I ran back to our house and packed a backpack. I had a little bit of money saved and I took that. I knew there was a bus that would go around the peninsula be-cause Grandma took me on it when I first came. It took a long time because it kept stopping to pick up people. I was scared someone would make me get off. But the bus finally got to Empire, and I got off. I walked the rest of the way here."

Maria lets out a long sigh, as if the telling of the story has worn her out.

Tara shivers at the thought of all the things that might have gone wrong with this plan. Being young has its advantages, like not knowing all the terrible things that could happen.

"You were very brave," is all she says. Then she has another thought. "What did your mom say?"

"She wants me to stay and help my grandma, but she did not know how bad grandma was after the stroke."

"You didn't tell her?"

"I don't want her to worry. She is so worried about the safety of my sister and so glad that I am safe staying here in America."

"Don't you think she would want to know what is going on with you?"

Maria's nods, but her voice quavers. "Probably. But I know she wants me to stay and go to high school in the States, so I have a chance of getting into college, maybe get a scholarship. I have to do well in school so I can get a good job and help my mom and my sister."

"That's a lot of responsibility. Maybe we should call her and let her know your grandma is recovering, that you are safe. Things will work out, you'll see."

Tara pulls the car into the driveway at her uncle's house. When he comes out onto the porch, Tara notices with surprise that he looks a bit disheveled. He and her aunt always looked neatly put together, whatever they were doing. She has not been paying enough attention, focused too much on her own grief. Uncle Robb watches her help Maria out of the car. Taffy races around the front yard, happy to be home and to have Maria here, for whom she seems to feel responsible.

"Hello. Looks like you had a little trouble with that ankle." Maria nods. "I'll bet you're hungry." He holds the door as Maria hops inside. Tara takes the backpack out of the trunk and follows them into the house.

Uncle Robb has already settled Maria in a comfortable chair with her foot resting on a footstool. She lays her head against the back of the chair and closes her eyes. Taffy sits beside her while Maria strokes the dog's soft ears.

"Rest for a few minutes and then you probably want a bath. We'll ice your ankle, and Uncle Robb and I will get some food together. Anything you don't like to eat?"

Maria shakes her head.

While Maria sleeps, Tara straightens up the extra bedroom which now has miscellaneous uses, and makes up the futon as a bed. She puts out clean towels in the second bathroom. When Maria wakes up, Tara helps her to the bathroom and leaves her to manage for herself, assuming that her presence would not be welcome. After a few minutes, she knocks on the door.

"Everything okay? Need anything."

"I am okay." Maria's voice is faint. "Almost done."

Tara goes into the kitchen where Uncle Robb is pulling ingredients out of the refrigerator to make dinner. He likes to cook for people and did much of the cooking for himself and Aunt Becca.

"It's a good thing you found her," Uncle Robb says quietly. "Taking the bus like that and walking all that way to stay in that old, abandoned house." He shakes his head. "The bad things that might have happened to her."

"I know. It's tough to be thirteen. Now, I have to talk to her grandma and see what she thinks about all of this. Do you know anyone at the hospital? I want to let her know Maria is okay. Find out if she is still in the hospital, what's the prognosis. Get her permission for Maria to stay with us."

"Let me think." Uncle Robb stops, looks out the window. "I think Jim, who I used to work with, has a daughter who works there as a nurse. I guess I could call him and see if she can help."

"Thanks. I will get Maria to call her grandma's cell phone first. If she answers, Maria can tell her where she is and find out how her grandma is doing."

Clean and wearing what was probably the last clean shirt she had, Maria stands in the doorway to the kitchen. She does not make eye contact with either of them. Tara helps her limp into the living room and hands her an ice pack to put on her ankle.

"I am thinking you could call your grandma's cell phone, see how she is doing, let her know where you are. I can talk with her and let her know who we are, find out what she wants to do."

Maria frowns.

"You are welcome to stay here if your grandma is not able to go home. But we have to do what she thinks is right."

Maria nods, frowning, and takes her phone out of her pocket. Tara stays in the kitchen and waits to find out where things stand. After a few minutes Maria calls to her, and she goes into the living room.

"Here, this nurse wants to talk to you." Maria has tears in her eyes. She thrusts the phone toward Tara.

The nurse at the rehab center explains that Maria's grandma needs a couple of weeks of therapy to regain her speech and movements. Mrs. Santos is still having difficulty speaking but is able to write a little.

The call goes back and forth. Mrs. Santos writes questions on a pad of paper, the nurse relays them, and Tara answers her questions. The nurse suggests that Tara and Maria come to the rehab facility as soon as possible to discuss what to do. Tara agrees and says she will bring Maria within an hour.

Maria takes the phone. "Grandma, I want to stay with Tara and Uncle Robb. They have been really nice to me. Please don't make me go stay with strangers. Tara and I are coming to see you so you can meet her." Maria's eyes tear up when her grandma struggles to answer. "I love you."

Uncle Robb calls Jim and briefly describes how Maria came to be with him. He asks if his daughter who is a nurse at the hospital could help by giving them a reference. Jim hangs up and calls back a few minutes later. His daughter Ann is at work today and will meet them at Grandma's room in one hour.

At the hospital they find the room where Maria's grandma is staying. Wearing her nurse's uniform, Ann is waiting for them. She stands in the doorway while Maria and Tara go in. Mrs. Santos looks frail and holds her mouth stiffly on one side. Maria runs to the bed and gently hugs her grandma.

Tara steps back while the two of them shed a few tears. Then she introduces herself and explains how she found Maria, how fearful Maria is of having to stay with strangers. She gestures to Ann, who comes in and tells Mrs. Santos that she has known Tara and Uncle Robb for a long time and can vouch for their characters.

Patiently, they continue the conversation with Grandma speaking a few words and scrawling a few more on paper. Mrs. Santos finally writes a big thank you, saying that she would be grateful if Maria could stay with Tara and her uncle. They agree that any major decisions regarding Maria will be discussed with her.

Tara put the address for Maria's grandma's house into her GPS and drives to it.

"That's it." Maria points to a small, two-story yellow house, with a porch across the front and a detached one-car garage at the end of a driveway. The yellow paint provides a colorful contrast to the pink hydrangea bushes along the front and the large pot of coral geraniums on the porch.

Tara parks the car in the driveway. She and Maria walk up three steps to the porch and Maria inserts her key in the lock.

"Maria. There you are. You gave me such a fright." The neighbor from across the street hurries toward them.

Maria turns in surprise. "It's Mrs. Barnes from across the street," Maria whispers to Tara.

"Hello, Mrs. Barnes. I'm Tara, and we've come to pick up some things for Maria." Tara waits to hear what Mrs. Barnes will say.

"I was out of town for a couple of days to help my sister, and when I got back, I went to visit your grandma. She has trouble talking, as you know, but she thanked me as best she could for looking after you. I did not know what she meant and did not want to alarm her, so before I left the hospital, I talked with the nurse. She told me that when your grandma was first admitted and you and I left at the same time, everyone thought you had come home with me. Then today you and Tara came to the hospital and made some arrangement for her to stay with you and your uncle. I did not know what to make of all that."

Maria looked down at her feet. "Sorry to alarm you."

"Oh, Mrs. Barnes. I think we met one time when I was with my aunt. You sometimes volunteer with the Cherry Festival."

Mrs. Barnes face beams. "Yes, I do." She peers closely at Tara. "Yes, I remember. You were about twelve then, I'd guess. Anyway, things seem sorted out now. So, no harm done. Well, I'll leave you to it. I'm here if you need anything."

"Thank you. You're very kind. Grandma is lucky to have such a good neighbor." Tara smiles at Mrs. Barnes.

Mrs. Barnes heads back across the street.

"Do you think she's being nosy?" Maria whispers.

"Could be. I'm sure she means well."

The rooms in the house are small and sparsely but comfortably furnished. Everything seems to be in place, except in the kitchen, where a few dishes were left when Grandma was taken to the hospital.

"My room is upstairs." Maria brushes tears from her eyes.

"Why don't you go up and pack what you need. We can always come back if you need other things. I will clean up the kitchen a bit." She pats Maria on the shoulder. "You and your grandma will be back home before you know it."

Maria nods and goes up the stairs.

Tara washes the dishes and wipes down the counter, then walks through the rest of the house while she waits for Maria. In the small study, she reads the titles of the books in a bookcase. Grandma seems to read a lot.

Back at Uncle Robb's house, Maria goes straight up to the room that Tara tells her has been set up for her.

"Everything go okay?" Uncle Robb looks at Tara.

"Her grandma needs a few weeks of therapy to regain her speech and motion. But fortunately, Jim's daughter Ann was there, and she spoke highly of us, assured the grandmother that Maria would be safe here. Her grandmother agreed that she could stay with us. I hope that is okay with you. I was not planning on a long stay, but I hate to turn her away. She seems to feel abandoned right now."

"We will manage. Looks like the poor lass is worn out."

In her room after Maria and her uncle have gone to bed, Tara takes out the journals. She looks forward to this time when she can join her aunt's adventures in France. Her own life seems to be getting more complicated instead of less.

Ten

Nice, France
1971

Vendredi, 5 Mars

It snowed last night! It's really cold in my room because we don't get much heat. And I only have sheets and two thin blankets on my bed. Wish I had a warm sleeping bag instead. Have to pretend I'm camping.

After classes we visited a sculptor's studio. He builds his sculptures with screws, horseshoes, boules, and other metal things. He has sold his work to famous people and seems to make a living this way.

After dinner two friends of Miguel's, one from Thailand and one from Latin America, brought guitars to the student café in the Cité. Edward, Paul, Marianne and Barbara also came. Miguel's friends are really talented. They play music from classical to popular. One of the songs popular with guitar players here is the theme song from the movie *A Man and a Woman*.

Miguel's friends talked me into playing my new guitar, but I am not as good as they are. It was fun, though. Students here from every country seem to love American music. I smoked my last cigarette. I decided I'd better quit smoking.

Lundi, 8 Mars

I am miserable. I have a really bad cold, and there is no place to go except this cold room. Marianne and Barbara brought me some soup from the Cité dining room, but they did not stay because they did not want to catch what I have. It is boring lying here with no TV or stereo, just a book to read. Mostly, I am sleeping anyway.

At dinner Marianne told Miguel that I am sick. When he heard that I am shivering from the cold, he brought me an extra blanket! He did not stay because he is not supposed to be in my room. I wanted to kiss him, but did not want to give him my cold. So, I kissed him on the cheek, and he smiled his beautiful smile. His brown eyes look so warm and kind when he smiles at me like that. The blanket is thick and super warm. And I am smiling because he is thinking about me! I hope I feel better tomorrow.

Mercredi, 10 Mars

Finally, I am mostly recovered from my cold. It was great to get out of this room! French class did not go well today because I had missed two days of classes and hadn't spoken French to anyone all that time. The professor was sympathetic that I was sick, but not sympathetic that my French was not better. I think I'm making progress, but sometimes it seems so slow. Sigh.

At the Faculte today, the fascists and gauchistes fought a battle of sorts. Someone threw a Molotov cocktail and burned part of the entrance, so the Faculte was closed! I don't understand how students could organize themselves as fascists. What a terrible thing to believe in. On the other side are the gauchistes, some of whom I think are Maoists. Then there is another collection of groups that work together to fight jail sentences and other issues. They all pass out a lot of propaganda, and many students admire the Black Panthers in the States.

I also found out today that Marianne is Jewish. No big deal, but she hadn't said anything before. She didn't say how she felt about the fascists being around, so I asked her. She told me that one set of her grandparents died in a concentration camp, and fascists have always made her nervous, but angry, too. I said I hope she knows we would defend her against the fascists anytime. She said thanks, but in France during World War II, one could not count on that. One never knows what they will do in that situation. I did not know what to say to that. I hope I would be brave enough to do the right thing.

She told me she had stayed on a kibbutz in Israel one summer, and she really liked it. She said Israel is special to her and she hopes to go back one day.

I can understand why Israel is important after the Holocaust. But I remember when I lived in the dorm, I listened to a presentation by a Palestinian student. He talked about the history of Palestine. When the Jewish people moved to Israel, his family was forced to leave the home that had been in their family for generations. I don't really understand why that happened. People should just live peacefully together. Why does one group of people take homes and land from another group of people?

Dimanche, 14 Mars

Yesterday, Barbara, Marianne, Paul, Edward and I took the train to Florence. First stop Ventimiglia, a transition from France to Italy. The border guard asked me if I had any hashish. Regrettably, I did not, ha, ha. Fortunately, he laughed and waved me through the gate. Making a joke, I guess.

We continued on the train to Genoa. Through the train window, the moon sparkled on the Mediterranean. Sometimes I can't believe I am really here. I never thought I would see the Mediterranean.

In Florence we found a pensione where we could stay. The workers are on strike at the art museum so we could not visit it! Tant pis! How disappointing. We had some good pizza and vegetables for dinner with a huge dish of chocolate and fraise ice cream for dessert. We walked through the flea market and around Florence to see the city. The streets seemed kind of dirty to me. But in the evening as we walked along the river, the buildings gleamed golden in the setting sun, clearly reflected in the water.

I wish Miguel was here! He had a paper that he needed to write, so he didn't come with us.

We rode a bus up into the hills to visit the olive groves which are in bloom and an old stone mill with a water wheel. Along the road we saw older women carrying baskets on their heads. In an old village with narrow, winding streets, we stopped at a restaurant for lunch. I wasn't sure what to order. I ordered a salad, but was disappointed to see that it was just lettuce. I didn't let on, just pretended I knew all along that's what it would be. The homemade ravioli was excellent, though, and I'm not usually fond of pasta.

Lundi, 15 Mars

At lunchtime Miguel told me he missed me over the weekend. He talked me into cutting class to walk to the park with him. Flowers are sprouting in the flowerbeds. Maybe spring is coming. We sat on a park bench close together and kissed. Then Miguel asked me if I had ever had sex. I was embarrassed to admit it, but I told him I hadn't. He told me that he is really attracted to me and asked me if I would ever want to have sex with him. I told him I would, even though I am nervous about it.

I told him that I am afraid of having sex because I am terrified of getting pregnant. What would I do?!! My parents would be horrified. I would have to drop out of school. And how would I support a baby, how would I take care of it? I would hate giving it away, not knowing if it would be loved and cared for properly.

Miguel says a woman friend of his told him there is a French doctor who speaks English who will prescribe birth control pills, no questions asked. He said he would make an appointment for me if I want him to. And I said yes! He smiled and gave me a big hug.

Now I am really nervous about the whole thing. What am I doing? What about Brian back home?

My roommate back in the States had sex for the first time just before Christmas. She said she was glad she did it, got her first time over with, but she is on the pill, so not so worried about getting pregnant. She told me that the pharmacist seemed to sneer at her when she filled her prescription for birth control pills. Was it because she didn't wear a wedding ring and, therefore, wasn't married? Or, did he think because she was young, she should want to have children? At home, I felt too embarrassed to get a prescription and go to the pharmacy to fill it. It's like announcing, "Hey, I'm having sex." Now I wish I had gone ahead and taken the pill.

My mom always stressed "saving yourself for marriage." I don't know if other girls, or young women, are doing that these days, but I don't think so. Still, having sex seems risky. During my senior year of high school, a girl in my class got pregnant at the beginning of the year. She dropped out of school and most people looked down on her, even other kids who I am sure were having sex but did not get pregnant. She kept the child, eventually went to night school and got her diploma, and later went to college. But it was not an easy life, I think.

I don't want to be in a position to be a single parent or give up a baby to strangers. I guess I'll figure things out. Everyone does eventually, I guess.

Mercredi, 17 Mars

Today was our first visit to the Tzigane community that we are studying to learn about their culture and the education of gypsy children in France.

We visited a Romany community who live in houses provided by the French government. The area is clean and the people seem relaxed. Each house has a TV. There are a couple of folkloric old wagons where the children seem to play. People also have house trailers for traveling on vacations.

Music is not considered a profession, but just part of life. Begging is rare. Leadership is not permanent, but fluid.

The school for the children is considered a gadjo (not Tzigane) school. We were told that when the children first start school, they are often 3 years behind, but catch up by age 10. They speak Romany at home, but learn French at school.

The men work as coppersmiths, making hammered metal flower pots and pitchers during the winter to sell to tourists in the summer. We visited one of the workshops and saw the beautiful things they make. I wanted to buy something, but had not brought any money.

After dinner we all went to a movie about Sacco and Vanzetti. I had never heard of them. They were Italian immigrants who were anarchists and union organizers in the States. In 1921 they were charged with committing robbery and murder at the Slater and Morrill shoe factory in South Braintree. They were found guilty, and even though a convicted murderer later confessed to participating in the crime with the Joe Morelli gang, they were executed in 1927.

In NYC, France, and around the world thousands of people demonstrated to protest the convictions and executions, which were based on prejudice against anarchists and immigrants, not evidence. The movie was an Italian-French co-production with song lyrics by Joan Baez.

Mardi, 23 Mars

At the café after lunch, I talked with one of the Moroccan students who is part of our group. He said he is an ex-Muslim. I found that interesting because my Algerian friend is a practicing Muslim and follows all the prayers and fasts that are part of his religion.

I saw the doctor today and got a prescription for birth control pills. Weird. I was really nervous and embarrassed. I'm not sure how I feel about taking the pill. Life is so complicated! Miguel met me afterward and asked me how I felt about it. He looked worried. I just said I did not know, and I did not feel like talking about it. He took me to a café and we talked about other things. Then he let me drive his Mobylette on the streets near the Cité. Great fun!

When I got back to the Cité, Marianne was excited because she had received a letter from one of her friends who is gay. He told her that on March 14th, gay liberation groups, between 2,500 and 3,000 people, marched on the state capital with a list of demands. I was surprised because I don't really know any gay people. But I think they should be treated as well as anyone else.

Jeudi, 25 Mars

Miguel has been wanting to go flying in a small plane, but it rained for a couple of days so we couldn't go. Today is sunny, so we went up in the plane. The view of the sea, mountains, and the countryside was spectacular, but the noise and the motion of the plane made me feel sick and dizzy. The pilot landed at a country airport and we stayed there for a few minutes. It was exciting to be in a small plane, but I did not feel well afterward, so that kind of spoiled it.

Miguel came to my room to type a paper. He had to sneak in and sneak out. We argued about whether life is pre-determined (as he thinks) or a series of choices that we make (as I think). We agreed to disagree. We played a game of chess, and he won. I learned to play by reading in an encyclopedia, so I guess it is not surprising that he won.

Tara closes the journal, stands up and walks to the window. Outside, it still looks like daytime with the moonlight glowing silvery yellow in the sky. She thinks about her aunt in France, on her own, trying to figure out her sex life.

It seems weird that taking birth control pills was such a big deal. Women she knows don't think much about it. It just makes life easier. The fear of getting pregnant is just as real now for many women as it was back then. Roe v. Wade recognized women's right to control their bodies in 1973, and now that recognition no longer exists for many women. She wonders if mothers still tell their daughters to "save it for marriage." Would their daughters pay much attention? Having sex outside marriage isn't such a big deal now.

Dorm life in France does not sound very comfortable. Having a cold with not enough heat. Weird to think of fascist and gauchistes students actually fighting on campus, although she knows there are fascists in this country. Sad to think that the Jewish-Palestine conflict has never been resolved, only gotten worse. People still suffer in Gaza and the West Bank.

Looks like her aunt's relationship with Miguel is heating up. He seems to look after her, and she seems to want to be with him. What about Brian? Did her aunt still write to him? Does he know about Miguel?

Tara's phone dings and she looks at the text message. Her half-sister, Riley.

"Hi, Riley."

"Hey, Tar." Tara smiles. Her stepsister Lauren could not say the name Tara when she was a one-year-old and always called her Tar. Later, when Riley was born, she called her Tar as well.

"When are you coming back here? I'm starting my senior year in the fall, and who's going to give me good advice? You will be here for my graduation in the spring, won't you? Oh, and how is Uncle Robb? Sad for him to lose Aunt Becca."

Tara texts back, "Don't worry. I'm just a text away. And I won't be gone long, just a few weeks. How's your summer going?"

They text back and forth for a few minutes, and then Riley leaves to meet her friends.

When Tara was growing up, her families felt so complicated. Choosing where to spend holidays and vacations, always trying not to offend anyone. Sometimes being an only child, sometimes living with two half-sisters, sometimes living with two stepbrothers. But it's still nice to know all of them are out there.

Eleven

Summer 2023

The next morning Maria comes downstairs and stands quietly in the kitchen doorway.

"You're up. I'm making pancakes, hope that's okay for you." Tara waves a turner toward the bowl of batter. Butter sizzles as she pours another spoonful of batter onto the griddle.

"It smells good. Can we visit mi abuela today?"

"Course. Your grandma may be sleeping a lot. Having a stroke takes a lot of energy out of people."

"I know, but I want her to know I am there. She is lonely for mi madre and mi hermana, just like I am since they had to go away."

"She will be glad to see you."

Uncle Robb comes into the kitchen. Tara thinks he looks as if he did not sleep very well. She knows he often wakes up, expecting to see Aunt Becca beside him, and finds she is no longer here.

"First ones are ready. Maria, could you find the maple syrup in the fridge?"

Maria opens the refrigerator, takes out the syrup and sets it on the table. Tara notes that the refrigerator looks bare. She and Uncle Robb have not been eating much lately. Time to get groceries and keep everyone fed.

They hear scratching at the back door, and Tara lets Taffy in. Uncle Robb fenced in the backyard when he and Aunt Becca had a dog, so Taffy has a safe place to run. The dog slurps up some water and then makes the rounds to say hello to the three people sitting at the table.

"Did you get Taffy when she was a puppy? I have always wanted to have a puppy." Maria reaches down to stroke Taffy's head.

"No, when we were all stuck at home so much during the pandemic, I decided to get a dog. I went to the Humane Society and there she was. She was a year old then, and had recently been left there by a family who could not afford to keep her. She looked at me with her big, brown eyes, and I knew I had to take her home."

"Poor Taffy. She knows how it feels to be abandoned by the people you love, just like me." Maria puts her arms around Taffy.

"We needed each other and have seen each other through some difficult times. She sticks pretty close to me." Tara smiles at Taffy

"You are both lucky." Maria leaves the table and goes upstairs to take a shower. She missed showers and being clean when she stayed in the Spencer farmhouse.

Uncle Robb stacks the plates and carries them to the sink. "Think she's okay?"

"Yes and no, I guess." Tara pauses. "Uncle Robb, I have a job interview today, at the toy store downtown. Do you feel okay being here with Maria?" Tara pours dish soap into the water.

"We'll manage." Uncle Robb pauses. "I can certainly take Maria to the hospital while you are gone."

Than "k you. I didn't want to ask. I should not be gone very long." Tara worries that she has put her uncle in a difficult position.

She goes upstairs and finds Maria dressed, sitting on her bed, staring out the window.

"Uncle Robb will be here if you need anything. There are books downstairs in the family room. Uncle Robb has a couple of streaming services if you want to watch something. You have your laptop. It looks like it will be a nice day if you want to sit outside." Tara grimaces. She thinks she sounds like a tour guide and is not sure any of it is helpful.

"I'll be okay." Maria looks up.

"And Taffy would probably enjoy having someone toss her ball for her to fetch."

Maria smiles then. "I could do that for her."

"Great."

When Tara arrives home from her job interview, Maria is sitting on the front porch, watching a boy mow the lawn. Taffy lies by her chair. The dog jumps up when she sees Tara and nudges Tara's hand with her head. Tara strokes the dog from her head to her tail.

"How was your day? Did you see your grandma?"

"I saw her for a little while. She can talk a bit now, but she fell asleep." Maria looks up at Tara. "Do you think my grandma is going to die?"

"No, the doctor says she just needs time and some help to recover. There may be things that she doesn't do as well. Like she might have some trouble remembering things. But she will be your grandma, just like before."

"I hope you're right."

"Don't worry. Things will work out."

"Did you get the job?"

"I did."

"Do you think you will like it?"

"I think it will be okay. Working with toys, you know. What's not to like?"

"That's true, I guess." Maria looks out at the yard. "Who is that boy mowing the lawn?"

"That's Jayden. He lives down the street and has been mowing Uncle Robb's lawn for the last couple of years." Jayden looks up from his mowing and Tara waves to him. He waves back.

The summer when she was 16 had been an especially difficult time for her. Her mom and stepdad argued a lot, and she worried they would get divorced. She didn't think she could take another divorce.

She convinced her mom to let her spend a lot of the summer with her aunt and uncle. Jayden's mom needed someone to care for Jayden and his older sister while she was at work, so Tara babysat for them. When Tara returned home at the end of the summer, things seemed to have calmed down between her mom and stepdad.

Jayden was only two years old that summer, so she does not know if he remembers much about that time. Tara was not around much since then, but she enjoyed watching him grow up whenever she came back to visit.

"How old is he?"

"I guess he must be fourteen or fifteen. I think he is going to be a sophomore next year." Tara looks at Jayden and realizes that he is pretty cute for a teenage boy. "You could maybe say hi to him when he finishes mowing. Uncle Robb always pays Jayden when he is done, so he will come to the house."

Maria shrugs. "I'm going to be fourteen next month."

"Oh, you're having a birthday soon. We will have to celebrate."

Tara goes around to the back of the house. Uncle Robb looks at the garden beds. Usually by now, there would be early crops ready to pick and small tomato and pepper plants beginning to grow. Tara sighs. Poor Uncle Robb. He seems so lost. He looks up at her as she comes closer, frowning.

"Does not look too good, does it?"

"That's okay. There has been a lot going on. There's always next year."

Uncle Robb shakes his head but does not comment.

"Thanks for taking Maria to see her grandma in the hospital. How did they seem?"

"The nurse said Grandma is improving. And when we were there, she made an effort to smile and reassure Maria that all would be okay. Maria tried to be brave, but I could see that she is worried. What will happen to her if her grandma can't look after herself, much less Maria?"

"I don't know. For now, let's just hope that all will be well. We'll figure something out."

When Tara is in the kitchen getting dinner ready, she hears voices on the porch. Uncle Robb has gone outside to pay Jayden for mowing the lawn. She hears him introduce Maria and then come back in. It is quiet for a few moments and then she hears voices that sound like Jayden and Maria talking.

After dinner Uncle Robb, Tara, and Maria sit on the back porch and watch the fireflies blink on and off across the yard. Crickets chirp in chorus through the night air.

"You are a citizen, but your mom and your sister are not? That must be very hard for all of you." Uncle Robb looks at Maria.

Maria looks down and does not answer at first.

"Yes, it's complicated. My parents were born in Mexico. They were married and had my sister. My grandfather died when my mom was little. My grandmother, who was also born in Mexico, moved to the States to live with a friend who told her she would be able to get a job here. While she was here, she married my second grandfather, who was a citizen, and so she became a citizen too.

"My father, mother and sister moved to the States to be near my grandmother, and I was born here in the U.S. We all went back for a few months to take care of my other grandmother, my dad's mother. After she died, we came back here because my mom thought my sister and me would be safer, and we could go to school, maybe go to college someday. But when they came back, my mom and dad and sister were still considered illegal.

"Last year ICE raided the place where my dad worked. They rounded up anyone without a valid work card, and he was deported. We really missed my dad. It was hard, but my mom still tried to keep the three of us here by working two jobs. She had to wear a tether and report in to some office. There was a lawyer who tried to help us, but it did not work out. And a month ago, mi madre and mi hermana were deported."

Tears trickle down Maria's cheeks. Uncle Robb reaches out and pats her arm.

"I am sorry. You are sad to be separated from them."

Maria nods and wipes her eyes.

"How long has your grandma lived up here?"

"Grandma and Grandpa lived next door to us in the mobile home park. And then Grandpa's friend called and said he should come up north because there was a good job available at one of the cherry orchards. He and Grandpa had been friends when they were kids, and their families picked cherries up north in the summers. So, my grandparents moved up here.

"We drove up to see them sometimes, but mi madre had to work a lot so we didn't come often. I was close to my grandparents, though, and we Skyped once a week, so they could keep up with what my sister and I were doing."

"Living up here must feel different from what you're used to."

"A lot different. I wanted to stay with my friend's family in Ann Arbor, but my mom wanted my grandma to be my guardian and take care of me until I finish high school." Maria gets up from her chair. "I think I will go to bed now."

Taffy gets up and nudges Maria's hand. Maria looks down and pets her.

"Do you need anything?" Tara watches Maria with concern.

Maria shakes her head. "No. I am fine."

Tara and Uncle Robb say goodnight and hope she sleeps well. After Maria goes up to her room, Tara looks over at her uncle.

"What do you think? Was I crazy to bring her here? I did not know what to do."

"No, you did the right thing. You couldn't leave her alone out there. She seems to trust you, and she definitely feels comfortable with Taffy." He smiles at the dog. "You are a great host." Taffy thumps her tail.

"Well, thank you for helping me out. I guess I will go in."

"You had a busy day. Goodnight. See you tomorrow."

Tara kisses her uncle's cheek and goes to her room. When she is ready for bed, she opens up her aunt's journal. She wonders what happened next.

Twelve

Nice, France
1971

Vendredi, 26 Mars

This morning my Algerian friend waited for me at the Cité and told me that he is going home to his family. His family misses him, and his brothers and uncle think the construction work is too hard for him. I think he is homesick, too. I told him I was glad to have met him and wished him well. He said the same, and gave me a big smile.

Today the five of us visited a French school. The class sizes at this school are smaller than in the States, I think, only about twenty students. They talked noisily to each other and fidgeted, as if they were not paying attention, but answered questions about the lessons when the teacher called on them. The teacher looks very young. The students seem to like him, even though they appeared not to be listening to him.

Some of the students at our dorm started circulating a petition to allow men to visit the women's dorm on weekends. A group of male students from Corsica (we were told they are fascists) argue against it. They claim they are trying to protect women, but most of us think we can take care of that ourselves. The concierge (Barbara calls him The Mechant because it means ill-natured) locks us in at night, and that just seems dangerous. What if there was a fire or some real threat? Not much protection!

I filled the prescription for birth control pills and started taking them. It felt weird when I gave the prescription to the pharmacist, but I guess I will get used to it. I could tell that Miguel is pleased I am taking them. I wish sex was easier, without worrying about pregnancy. One advantage of "saving it for marriage" I guess. Men are lucky they don't have to worry about it, and if a girl gets pregnant, it's her responsibility. Although sometimes the guy has to marry her (a shotgun wedding, they say). Sounds awful for both of them, unless they really love each other.

Mardi, Avril 6

The U is closed this week for Easter vacation, so yesterday Miguel and I started to hitchhike to Madrid. A friend Miguel met at the Cité has an apartment there, and he said we could stay for the weekend because he will be visiting friends. Wow! An apartment with a real bathroom and a kitchen and sitting area. What luxury!

We got a ride to Arles and checked out the Roman ruins as we walked through the village. I enjoyed the cheerful yellow dandelions that bloom along the roadside. Must be spring! A businessman gave us a ride to Narbonne. In Narbonne there so many students on break who were hitchhiking that there was actually a long line of hitchhikers on the edge of town!

Finally, a truck driver stopped for us and we made it to Perpignan. We took a bus to the French-Spanish border and got a ride with a man who talked about girls as sexual partners and Americans who don't wear bras. He asked me if I had yet slept with a Frenchman, and if I wanted to!! I pretended that I did not understand what he said, and Miguel told him that American girls are not like that. I was glad when that driver dropped us off!

We got another ride to the border and walked across into Spain. Then we took a train to Madrid. We rode third class on wooden bench seats which were very uncomfortable. But the people sitting with us were friendly. Naturally, Miguel spoke to them in Spanish and got along great with everybody. The scenery changed from craggy, red cliffs and bare plains, to green spaces, and then to desert grayness. Small herds of sheep grazed in the fields, and irrigation watered the farms.

The Madrid apartment is great, and we were able to cook our own dinner and take showers. Heaven! We both eyed the double bed in the bedroom and felt a bit shy. We had been waiting to be alone like this, but we felt awkward.

Miguel confessed that he was not a virgin but had not had much sexual experience, and I reluctantly admitted that I had very little. We took our time, and Miguel was very kind. After we undressed each other and began to explore the bodies we had never seen before, I lost some of my nervousness.

Afterward, we lay close together and held hands. We both grinned because it had been awkward at first, but we had finally really been together, and we felt pleased with ourselves and with each other. It felt wonderful to fall asleep cuddled up beside him.

Mercredi, 7 Avril

We slept in this morning. It was tantalizing to think that we could have sex whenever we wanted. After breakfast we went to the bullfighting arena and museum, The Museo Taurino, where we viewed replicas and paintings of famous toreadors and bulls, with elaborately embroidered capes and other regalia. The bullring is an impressive large, round stone space with entry arches all around the outside edge. All seems very weird to me, a very different cultural phenomenon. Miguel really wants to see a bullfight and I agreed, but I am uneasy about it.

In the afternoon we went to the Prado. Goya's paintings are bright with color and full of passion. I was intrigued by the 3rd of May painting because that is my birthday. Actually, it is a painting depicting the rebellious people who were executed by the French army at the end of the war with Napoleon. Not a very cheerful scene for my birthday!

The El Greco paintings are very different, pastel colors and full of light. I think Goya seems more down to earth, full of humanity, while El Greco exhibits more a sense of spirituality. We plan to go to Toledo where El Greco lived and painted. I think it's funny that he is considered a Spanish painter, but he was actually was born in Crete and was called "the Greek".

We went out to a restaurant to eat paella, a specialty of Spain. Miguel considered it a real treat, but I was not so enthused about the seafood still in the shells.

Jeudi, 8 Avril

Today we relaxed in the morning and then went to Retiro Park where we rented a canoe and then a paddle boat to cruise around the pond. We bought ice cream and sat on a bench to watch the families enjoy a Saturday afternoon. There is nothing like parks to cheer your heart in the city!

In the evening we walked around Madrid and encountered a large group of people who seemed to be waiting for something. Miguel asked one of them what they were waiting for, and they said the Maundy Thursday parade was coming. Pretty soon, a group of soldiers mounted on beautiful white horses rode down the street. After them came the repenters of sin in black monks' robes, with wide burlap belts and tall, black hats with veils over their faces. Some walked barefoot and lugged wooden crosses, while others carried long yellow candles.

Many people, including children, followed behind them, all dressed up in their best clothes or wearing white robes. Next came a float with a figure of Christ surrounded by lots of lighted candles and colorful flowers. Last of all, the float of the Virgin Mary, brightly lit with numerous candles. People clapped and cheered for the two floats. I have never seen anything like this!

Sex is much easier now, and it has been a wonderful day!

Vendredi, 9 Avril

We took the train to Toledo, a small city with crowds of people visiting the sites. An old stone castle sits on the hill overlooking the town. At the Church of Santo Domingo, we admired El Greco's famous altarpiece paintings. His use of light is very delicate and ethereal. The paintings are very beautiful, and many people came to see them, probably because it is Easter time. He is also buried here.

The Museo de Santa Cruz is in a 16th century building with fine arts, archaeology, and decorative arts. The entrance is an ornate, decorative façade in a Spanish method called plateresque.

We saw the Alcázar, an historic fort where the fascists held out in a battle with the Republicans during the Spanish Revolution. Miguel talked a lot about the Spanish Civil War. Too bad the fascists won in the end.

Later in the day we met a Japanese woman who was visiting Spain on her way home from attending university in the States. She shared her first-class train seat with us, and when we got back to Madrid, we all went out for paella.

Dimanche, 11 Avril

When I woke up this morning, I heard the church bells peal from the cathedral next door to the apartment building. It was a lovely chiming sound, a bit loud, though.

Today was bullfight day. I was nervous about seeing the bullfight and didn't really enjoy it. It was much more dangerous for the matadors (there were 3 of them and 6 bulls) than I thought it would be, but mostly I just felt sorry for the bulls. They didn't deserve to be treated like that. One bull gored an assistant, broke the fence, knocked over a horse, and then gored the matador! But all the bulls were killed in the end. Miguel told me that the meat is donated to charity. I don't think that makes it better to kill the bulls. An interesting cultural phenomenon, but not for me!

It is Easter Sunday, and I wonder if the Easter Bunny comes to Spain with Easter baskets. I didn't see any evidence of that in the shops. I wonder if that is just a custom in the U.S. or if anywhere else has an Easter Bunny. Even though at home most people I know go to Easter services, everyone here seems more serious about Easter.

Mercredi, 14 Avril

Our last day in Madrid. We took the subway out to the country and walked all over, looking for a place to ride horses. Miguel was really determined to ride one. I haven't ever ridden a horse before, just a pony at the fair, but I was willing to give it a try. The countryside was green and beautiful, but It turned out that the ranch we were looking for was private, so we took the bus back to Madrid. We got the Teleférico out to the amusement park where we took a ride through the fun house and then went into the Mouse, a slanted, distortion experience.

Tomorrow we will hitchhike back to Nice. We talked about what would happen to us then. We do not have a private place where we can be together in Nice the way we want to be. And after these few days, and how wonderful we felt, it will be hard. We did not talk about the arguments we have had. I think we both want to forget that part. Will that work? I wonder.

Vendredi, 16 Avril

Before leaving Madrid yesterday, we ate a great breakfast of freshly squeezed orange juice and toast made with thick, homemade bread. We had to wait a long time to get a ride out of the city, but were picked up by a truck driver who said he could take us to Barcelona where we would find a truck driver to give us a ride to Nice. In Barcelona, we ate a delicious dinner with him, but then we had to sit up all night in a café because there was no room at the hotel where he stayed. I was so tired and felt a bit sick.

We were tired of waiting, so we started hitchhiking again, but it took too long to get a ride. We took a train to Figueras and stayed there overnight. Miguel and I argued a lot about silly things. Maybe because the trip was so frustrating and tiring. I hope it doesn't mean we aren't going to be together when we get back to Nice.

Samedi, 17 Avril

Miguel and I argued again this morning. He is so domineering sometimes!

We rode the train to Perpignan. A little girl on the train showed me her nursery rhyme cards in Spanish. Very fun. Miguel and I shared a box lunch because we did not have much money. We had to wait three hours in Perpignan to get a ride to Montpellier, and then we had to wait in the dark to get a ride. Finally, we took a train to Nice. And we are home (what is home for now anyway).

Dimanche, 18 Avril

Miguel and I spent the day at the Cité library. We both have papers that are due in a couple of weeks, and we haven't spent as much time as we should on them. I am glad that my French is pretty good now, because I have lots of reading to do in French in order to finish my research on the education of gypsy children in France. Miguel helped me whenever I got stuck on a French word or phrase.

The Cité doesn't serve supper on Sundays, so some of us walk down to the café at the bottom of the hill and order omelettes, frites, and pêches Melba. The omelettes are always delicious, and the frites are made with fresh potatoes. Although the pêches Melba are made with canned peaches, they are served with ice cream so they still taste like a treat.

At the café, I am learning to play pinball. Some of the French students who come in are very good at it. They give us tips on how to do it better. You are not supposed to shake the machine too much because then you get a TILT message and your game stops. We all found that out, and now we are more careful, just a gentle nudge will do.

Mardi, 20 Avril

Today was our second visit to the Tzigane community. We visited the part where the Sinti live. In their workshop they weave beautiful baskets to sell.

The children seem very free to run around and do what they want. Parents are not authoritarian, unlike French parents, I am told. Two girls that I spoke with were talkative and noisy. They spoke French fluently, as well as their language, Romani, and demonstrated that they had also learned some English. They were interested in us and asked a lot of questions. Where do you live? Is it hot or cold there? Is it better than here? How far is it? Did you come by car or train? They wanted us to sing American songs, and taught us some Sinti phrases. They liked our short skirts.

After supper Barbara and Marianne found a jar of peanut butter in a gourmet shop and brought it back to the Cité with a jar of jam and a baguette. None of us have seen peanut butter since we arrived in France, so we all had a PB & J party! Very funny.

Marianne told us she met two American students while she was drinking a coffee after lunch. They are traveling around Europe, and they told her that students continue to stage sit-ins at U.S. campuses. On April 15 delegations of students who are upset because there are not many black students admitted to the University of Florida had a sit-in to protest. The President of the University wouldn't even meet with them and had a lot of them arrested and put on academic probation. We all thought that was unfair.

Vendredi, 30 Avril

I turned in my report on the Education of Tsiganes in France and went to the beach. I saw a French girl I had met before, so we hung out together and bought beignets
at the food stand for lunch. We took turns speaking French and English, because she wanted to practice her English and I wanted to practice my French. The weather is already warm, and it felt great to soak up some sun.

Paul said his cousin is in the Navy, and his ship is docked nearby. He wanted to go and see him, so he borrowed a car. Barbara, Miguel and I went with him. I wasn't sure how I felt about the Navy, given they are part of the military.

On the way there, we spotted a submarine docked in port. Paul parked the car and went over to talk to the guys standing by the sub, because he wanted to see what the inside of a sub was like. The sub guys said the guys couldn't go in, but the girls could. So, Barbara and I actually toured a submarine. Can't say I understood much about how things work, except that it was very tight quarters with lots of humming machinery, and I don't think I could ever do what those sailors do. They were all really nice to us, very polite.

When we got to the ship where Paul's cousin is stationed, we were allowed on the deck. We talked to his cousin and several of the other sailors. This was a downtime for them, and they were eager to talk.

On the way home, Paul told us that a couple of the sailors asked him if he knew where they might get some marijuana, and he told them he had some. We did not know about it, but one of the American students that we are friends with was heading home to the States and could not take his stash with him, so he gave it to Paul. The sailors said they will come to the Cité tomorrow evening and buy it from him. The Navy guys seem okay. I can't imagine them killing people.

Tara stops and goes back to reread about the trip to Madrid. She feels like she is reading about someone other than Aunt Becca. She never really thought about her aunt having sex, and certainly not with anyone other than Uncle Robb. Of course, it's absurd because she herself has had sex with more guys than just Kyle. She feels embarrassed to be reading what her aunt has written. And part of her feels happy for her aunt, that she was finally able to relax about sex and not be so worried about it.

It must have been fun that students could hitchhike all over and feel safe. Tara has never hitchhiked because she never felt safe doing it.

The Maundy Thursday parade seems spectacular. So religious! At first Tara thought there might be a video of it, but laughs at herself. No cell phones back then. Would have made a good selfie!

The bullfight sounds terrible. She is surprised that her aunt was willing to attend such an event, but she was open to new experiences, which is usually a good thing.

And she is amazed that her aunt toured a submarine and visited a Navy ship.

Reading about her aunt's adventures makes her want to start traveling again. Where would she want to go? A safari to Africa to see interesting animals? A trip to Japan? A visit to Morocco with maybe a ride on a camel? So many choices.

Thirteen

Summer 2023

Tara looks in her closet for something to wear on her first day at work. This is clearly a good time to look for a job as there are lots of openings, and she got a call for an interview soon after she applied for the job. She is eager to earn money so she will have something to start her life over with.

Unsure what to wear, she tries on a couple of pairs of pants and discards a couple of shirts as either too casual or too dressy. She decides on a nice pair of pants and a short-sleeved flowered shirt. Casual, but not too casual. Looking at herself in the mirror, she decides she will just view this as a new experience. After all, what could be better than stocking toys and helping kids find what they want?

In the kitchen she cuts a slice of bread and puts it in the toaster. Uncle Robb has already made coffee, so she pours a cup. A rinsed-out empty cereal bowl sits in the sink. Must be Maria's. She hears Maria's voice and Taffy's bark. Looking out the window, she sees that Maria is already tossing the ball for the dog.

In the living room her uncle stands by the window and watches the bird feeder that hangs from a birch tree outside. Several bright yellow goldfinches gleam in the sunshine that filters through the leaves on the tree. She is pleased that he decided to fill the feeder again, but worried about how he will spend the day.

"Uncle Robb, I am on my way downtown to the toy store. Don't want to be late for my first day of work. I am feeling a bit nervous, so am going to walk there. It's a bit far, but the exercise will feel good."

"You'll be fine there. Don't work too hard." He offers a wan smile.

"Will you be okay?" Tara had been so set on finding a job that she hadn't really thought about how he would cope on his own.

"Of course. I'll be fine. Not the first time in my life that I've been on my own."

"I know." Maybe she is hovering too much. He has never been weak and dependent.

"Looks like Maria is up and already playing with Taffy."

"She loves that dog. We'll go and see her grandma a bit later."

"Thanks for doing that."

"No problem." Tara waves and walks out the door.

Random clouds drift across the bright sun in the intense blue sky. Colorful pots of flowers on porches or planted in gardens along the front walkways burst in a splash of color against the green lawns. Some of the people she meets on the streets say hello or nod to her.

Tourist season has started. The main street is already clogged with groups of people who amble along and gaze into store windows or stop in the middle of the sidewalk to discuss where to eat. Tara dodges them with a few mumbles of excuse me and reaches the toy store.

At the register, the store manager places two Lego sets into a bag. She looks up when Tara enters and gestures for her to come over while she wishes the customer a good day.

"Glad you're here. We're already busy, and Cindy couldn't make it in today, so it's just Marcy and me. This is Marcy." She gestures to the woman at the register who is already ringing up another sale.

"Hi, Tara."

There is no time to chat with her co-worker. The manager leads her down one of the aisles

"I'll show you around the store and where we keep extra stock. Then you can shadow Marcy who will show you how to ring up purchases and explain how things work at the register. I won't put you on the register until you have had enough time to get used to what's required."

Tara follows the manager around the store and listens to her explain about the many kinds of toys that are organized by age groups. During the rest of the day, she spends time at Marcy's side at the register and helps a few customers who are looking for specific toys. She is surprised to see some of the same toys that she played with when she was growing up. There seem to be a lot more kinds of Lego sets, though. She imagines what it would feel like to open all the toys and try them out.

At the end of the day, she doesn't feel especially successful. She caught onto how to work the register, but there are lots of things to remember, and sometimes people interrupt her in the middle of a sale to ask a question. She still doesn't know where everything is or what toys are available in the store when people ask her where to find something. The manager thanks her and tells her it will all get easy eventually.

She walks back to Uncle Robb's house, enjoying the warmth of the summer day and the scent of flowers and recently mown grass. The sun occasionally peeks through the white haze that covers the sky. When it succeeds, shadows dance through the leaves of the trees that line the sidewalk. In spite of being tired from all the new information to remember, she is pleased to have a job and earn some money again.

Uncle Robb sits on the front porch. He looks up and smiles when he sees her. She wonders if he has been waiting for her.

"How did it go? First day on the job is always a bit stressful, I think."

"Everyone was nice, but I felt inadequate. I'm used to knowing what I'm doing and just getting at it. But everything was new. I know it will get easier. What did you do today?"

"Bill stopped by to see how I was doing. It was kind of him, but I still find it hard to talk to people. They mean well, but I feel like they really hope I am getting over it. Of course, no one ever really gets over grief like this, but we often feel uncomfortable around other people's grief, I guess."

"Yeah. I feel that way, too. All my friends are nice about it, but they want me to be over it and act like I was before. Except Amber. She lets me have my grief, if I want to. Is Maria here?"

"She took Taffy for a walk. Hope that's okay."

"Course." It is okay, but it makes Tara nervous. Has Maria ever walked a dog before?

As if reading her mind, her uncle says, "I had her walk around the backyard for a while with Taffy on a leash to get used to it. Taffy was well-behaved for her. I told her just to go around the block."

"Okay."

"She may not make it that far. Jayden might be home from mowing lawns."

"Ah, I see."

That evening, Tara is tired from her first day of work, but feels restless. She picks up her aunt's journal. Reading it has become a welcome escape from worries about where her life is going. It's reassuring that her aunt was trying to figure things out and her life turned out well.

Fourteen

Nice, France
1971

Lundi, 3 Mai

Today is my 21st birthday! A dreary, rainy day. I tried to catch a bus, but it pulled out into the street just as I got to the bus stop. I had to sit and wait for the next one and my feet got wet. I went to class about gypsies in France, and no one said happy birthday.

I am starting to tire of palm trees. I long for the hardwood trees of Michigan that leaf out bright green in the spring and turn brilliant colors in the fall.

After class I sat in my room and watched the rain drizzle down the window. I didn't feel well, so I took a nap. If I were back home in the States, there would be lots of celebrating. Turning 21 in the States means you can drink legally. Actually, I probably wouldn't have wanted to get drunk anyway.

The 21st
Twenty-one,
The magic of rain.
Celebrate
the nothingness it brings,
loneliness, and other things.

Later in the day the students on my program came to my room to wish me happy birthday, and we all went to supper together. It did not feel like a special day. After dinner, Edward invited us all to his room. Everyone seemed restless, talking a lot and subtly watching the door. Finally, when Miguel arrived with a cake he had made, everyone yelled surprise and sang a loud happy birthday song. A couple of students walking by the room peeked in, so we invited them to have cake with us.

It was a surprise party, so my friends had kept it a secret all day. I loved it that Miguel organized the party and made a cake, but I wish I had known because I felt so lonely during the day. The cake was delicious, and we drank wine and talked and played charades and the day was better. And now I'm 21. How did I get so old?

Dimanche, 9 Mai

Yesterday I got three letters from home. One was from my sister telling me what she has been doing, reminding me of familiar things back home. My roommate sent me an article about the Mayday action in Washington, D.C., a big antiwar protest. The protesters really stopped business in the city. But the Nixon Administration called in the National Guard. An estimated 12,000 people were locked up, the largest mass arrest in U.S. history! I kind of wish I had been there. I could have celebrated my birthday protesting the war in Vietnam.

I also got a letter from Brian. He misses me and is looking forward to my return home next month. I miss him, but how can we be the same now? And what if I decide not to go home for the summer?

What about Miguel? He wants me to stay here while he finishes his degree, and then he wants us to get married and go back to Latin America. It sounds so adventuresome and intriguing. And I do love him. But I have doubts.

I remember baking cookies on a rainy Sunday afternoon. Picnics, sailboats, roasting hotdogs and smores. Hanging out with friends, playing guitars. At home, life seemed simpler. When I return, I don't think I will be the old me. Too many things have changed. Who will I be? Will anyone know me?

Should I leave my old life behind, stay and build a new life, one I have never known before? Stay or go? Return home or make another life? I would miss my mom and dad and sister if I lived in Latin America. Would I even fit in there?

Yesterday, I received a letter from one of my former roommates. She and her boyfriend are getting married next Saturday. She said she wished I was there, so I could be in the wedding party. I wonder how she already feels so sure that this guy is the right one, the one she wants to spend her life with. Wish I could decide so easily.

Mardi, 11 Mai

I went for an early walk this morning for some peace and quiet to think. The stores were just opening as the shopkeepers pushed up the metal grates that cover their shops during the night. An elegant pâtisserie caught my eye. The ones closer to the dorm are casual and plain. But these windows were full of elaborate displays of sugared fruit, colorful mounds of slices of oranges, lemons and pineapple.

I do not often buy sweets from the pâtisseries, because I am careful about how much money I spend. We get a small allowance each month while we are on the study program. Since I used up most of my savings to pay for the airfare to get to Europe, the allowance is all the money I have to spend for the month. But I couldn't resist and went in just to look. I bought a mille-feuille (Marianne says in the States they are sometimes called Napoleons). They set it in a small, white box.

On my way home, I sat on a bench by the beach and watched the waves lap the shore while I bit into the flaky pastry with creamy filling. Worth every franc. I started to think about Miguel. What if I did come back in a few months? To finish a degree in teaching I need to complete one more semester of classes at the U and complete one semester of student teaching. In one semester I might have enough credits to get a degree. I could skip the student teaching.

I'm really not sure that I want to teach. In high school when I asked the school counselor or my parents what else I could do, they didn't have any ideas. My dad thought teaching was a great idea. So did my mom, and she didn't want me to be a secretary. I definitely didn't want to be a nurse. I must be capable of doing something, but what? I don't really know any women in my town with a college degree who are doing anything but teach.

Suddenly, people sitting on the beach shouted and pointed to something out in the water, bobbing on the waves. I watched as it rolled in closer and gasped. It was a head! I didn't know what to think. I followed other people who rushed down to the edge of the water and watched this head roll in to shore. We all let out our breath. It was only from a mannequin! I wonder what we would have done if it had been real.

Vendredi, 14 Mai

Marianne and I decided to take the train to Geneva today and spend the weekend. We both wanted to visit Switzerland and see the Alps. We did get to see the Alps. In fact, the train stopped right in the middle of nowhere, where we had a fantastic view of the Alps rising up on both sides of us with peaks of glistening white snow, and we had to get off the train!

The air smelled fresh and clean, and it was very quiet with no highways or towns nearby. We were really worried when the train took off without us, but the other passengers reassured us that the train always stops here, and another train would pick us up. And pretty soon another train came along and we got on it. We never did understand why this happened.

Anyway, we finally arrived in Geneva, a lovely city nestled in the mountains on its own large lake. We found a room in a small hotel, ate fondue for dinner. At first, we didn't know that we had to also order food to dip into the cheesy fondue sauce, but the waiter suggested that would be a good idea. So, we ordered bread and vegetables to dip into the cheese and small cubes of meat to dip into hot oil.

On Saturday we went inside several stores that sold watches and clocks. I have never seen so many different kinds. I bought a small clock for my sister. She hates to get up early in the morning, and the clock has a special alarm bell with a clapper, so maybe she won't mind hearing it so much. In the park there is a giant clock made up of flowers with a clockwork inside, so it actually keeps time.

We rode the ferry around Lake Geneva and went past the Jet d'Eau, a fountain erected in 1886 that can shoot up to 140 meters! In the distance we viewed the Alps and Jura Mountains, including Mont Blanc.

On Sunday we took the train back to Nice. We sat in a compartment with only one occupant, a girl who looked about thirteen. We said hi, but she seemed very shy and mostly read or looked out the window. Then this weird man came in. He kind of leered at all of us, at least that's how it felt to me, and he made moaning sounds at times. Marianne and I looked at each other, wondering if we should go to another compartment. But we didn't want to leave the young girl alone with him, so we stayed.

This time the train did not stop in the middle of nowhere but continued on to Nice. Miguel met me at the train station. I had really missed him!

Vendredi, 28 Mai

Hurray! Our sociology classes are over. Just one more week of language classes. Then we are on our own to travel elsewhere or to go home. Most of the American students that I know plan to travel when the semester is over. It would be a shame to go home without seeing as many different places as I can. I don't know when or if I will ever be back in Europe. I hope I will.

Miguel and I plan to hitchhike around England, Scotland, and Wales and camp along the way. I am really excited to see all of those places! Miguel still has one more week of classes, too. After our classes are over, we will just hang out in Nice for a week to finish things and pack. Then we will take off. Miguel has a tent and a sleeping bag, and I am going to buy a sleeping bag from a student who is going home.

Two weeks ago, I wrote to my parents to tell them I am going to hitchhike with Miguel this summer instead of coming home at the first of June. I think they will not be pleased. I know they miss me and want me to come home. I also know that they will be worried that I am having sex (I am), and they think sex is only for people who are married. It seems like everyone is having sex these days, but my parents don't know that.

After lunch today when I was waiting for Marianne to walk back to the Cité, a male student from Africa walked up to me. He said he was going back to Africa tomorrow and asked me if I wanted to come with him. I had never met him before! I just said no, I don't think so.

Dimanche, 6 Juin

One of our French teachers organized an end-of-school-year party at her family's cabin up in the mountains. It was a wooden two-story cabin with stones along the bottom half. Inside, a table was covered with food. Meat, of course, as the French are fond of meat. But there were also delicious breads, cheeses, fruit, hors d'oeuvres, wine. People mostly talked in French, but some of them also spoke English. I spoke French all day. I played a French card game and understood it. It was fun learning the rules in French and following along.

All of us on our program feel kind of sad. We might not have all been friends if we hadn't met here, but we have been together and depended on each other for five months. We might never see each other again.

Mardi, 8 Juin

Miguel borrowed a car from a friend so that he, Paul, an American woman we met named Sandy who is traveling around France, and I could drive to Saint-Tropez and go skinny-dipping. It is so remarkable that this is acceptable in Saint-Tropez, even in the daytime!

Just out of the town we set ourselves up on some large, flat rocks that cluster along the shore. I was afraid I would feel too shy when we got there, but I didn't. It felt okay since all of us took off our clothes. Paul grabbed my camera and took a picture of me topless. I do not think I will get it printed.

It was a lovely, sunny afternoon. We lay on the warm rocks in the sun, and when we felt hot we slid into the water and swam around. The Mediterranean was calm, and the water felt smooth and warm. Later in the afternoon we got dressed and stopped at a café in Saint-Tropez for something to eat.

Tara feels a bit shocked by the last entry. She can't imagine her aunt going skinny-dipping with friends. She thinks of her aunt as being adventuresome, but dignified. Another side to her aunt.

She hadn't realized that the movement against the Vietnam War was so militant, or had so much support. She knew her aunt and uncle had been part of the movement and were proud of that, but not how extensive the movement had been.

Aunt Becca's career options were pretty limited, yet her aunt was so smart, she could have done anything. More careers are open to women now, but it is still hard to decide what to do.

What must Brian have thought when Aunt Rebecca didn't come home at the end of her semester abroad? He must have wondered if she was going to break up with him. He probably didn't hear from her for most of the summer. How did he feel about that?

Tara suddenly remembers the clock that Aunt Becca brought back from Europe for her mother, her aunt's sister. It always sat on her mother's nightstand, even though she didn't use it anymore for an alarm. Tara had been fascinated that it had to be wound regularly in order to keep time. Sometimes, her mother let her set the time, wind up the clock, and listen to the soft clanging of the alarm.

She leans back against her pillows. Has she made the right choice in bringing Maria home with her? What is she going to do at the end of the summer? What if she just drifts along until she finds herself turning forty without a career or a relationship or any direction to her life?

Out the window dark clouds gather in the northern sky, and she feels the change of pressure, the heaviness of the air. She turns out the light and tries to sleep.

Fifteen

Summer 2023

Tara wakes up with a headache. She turns over, shifts her pillow to a new position, and tires to go back to sleep. It's only 6:00 in the morning, and she feels like she has been awake all night. In the midst of her own grief and feelings of loss, she feels responsible for her uncle and now for Maria. What has she gotten herself into?

At least she doesn't have to go into work today. Since she can't sleep, she decides that a hike will help her to put things in perspective. Taffy wakes up and puts a paw on the bed.

"Did I wake you up? Feel like an early morning hike?"

Taffy wags her tail. Always willing to go along with a hike.

Tara opens her door and listens. All is quiet. Uncle Robb and Maria must still be asleep. Quietly, she gets dressed, grabs a muffin, fills a water bottle, and leaves a brief note.

Thin clouds cover the sky after the storm that passed through in the night. On the horizon, the sun peeks out in a thin strip of blue sky.

Tara turns the car left when she sees the sign for the lake trail. She carefully maneuvers the car around the ridges and potholes as her Subaru bumps down the road to the gravel parking lot. One other car is parked in the small area. She lets Taffy out of the back and walks over to the entrance sign. The map is faded, but she can see that the trail meanders along a stream down to the lake and then loops around the lake back to the stream trail. Impossible to get lost.

"Okay, Taffy. This is the second of Aunt Rebecca's favorite hikes. I came here with her on a hike once. I started hiking with her when I was old enough to walk on my own. Always a special time, with surprise snacks and discoveries of wildflowers and animal tracks. I still have some of the different colored bird feathers and special stones I picked up back then."

Taffy looks up at her and grins, it seems to Tara. Tara laughs. "You're a good listener. Okay, let's go."

She follows the trail along the creek, stops to listen to the gurgling waterfalls that ripple over the fallen logs. She closes her eyes and lets the sound of rushing water wash over her.

Near the bridge where the stream rushes out of the lake, Tara admires a dam built from a disorderly pile of logs. Behind the log dam, the lake water rises higher, some of it rushing through gaps in the dam into the stream. Beavers, she remembers. It would be fun to see them, but Aunt Becca told her they come out more often in the evening than in the afternoon.

She snaps on Taffy's leash in case they meet people on the trail, and turns down the path on the right side of the lake. She spots a few bunchberry flowers, their white blossoms perched in the middle of lime green leaves.

Large and small roots crisscross the trail, reminding her to watch her feet. If she had four feet like Taffy, she could bound over the roots like there was nothing to it. She follows the curve away from the lake and into the trees for a short distance, and then she spies the lake again. On the edge of the trail, a few coral and yellow, lantern-shaped flowers of columbine hang from tall stems.

She and Taffy step carefully along two boards lying side by side across a muddy patch of the trail. A narrow wooden bridge spans another creek that empties into this end of the lake.

Halfway across the short bridge, Tara stops to watch waterfalls cascade over the stones in the stream. She breathes deeply, aware of the sadness that seems to cling to her since the pandemic, her aunt's death, and Kyle's leaving.

She chooses seven stones with colored stripes that she took from her aunt's collection. At one side of the creek, she builds a small cairn underneath a large oak tree.

"In remembrance of Aunt Becca," she says. "Thank you for all the things you taught me. For all the times you listened when I needed someone to talk to. For all the love and support you offered me."

At the intersection of the trail, she stops suddenly and grabs Taffy's collar. A porcupine sits in the center of the trail. Taffy spots it and stands still, nose sniffing the air. The porcupine slowly moves its front paws up and down.

"Looks like he's doing tai chi." Tara smiles.

The porcupine spots Taffy and scurries off into the bushes. At an opening in the trees, Tara watches a group of birds drifting across the water. Black and white. Mergansers?

Completing the loop around the lake, they cross a larger bridge across the creek. Tara keeps Taffy on the leash to keep her from rushing down the trail into the water.

In the parking lot, the other car has left, and they met no one else on the trail. Solitude comforts her, not having to smile and say hello, not having to pretend that everything is all right.

When Tara arrives home from hiking, she hears laughter and walks around to the back of the house. Taffy picks up her ball from the ground and drops it on Tara's foot. Tara picks it up and tosses it toward the back fence. Taffy dashes after it, brings it back, and drops it again.

Maria kneels in the garden while Uncle Robb picks up another tomato plant from a cardboard box. He smiles at Tara.

"Nice walk?"

"We had it to ourselves. It reminded me of Aunt Becca. I built a cairn out of some of the rocks, so a part of her spirit will always be there."

He nods.

"Look Tara. I planted two rows of beans. If I planted the bean seeds right, they will come up in a few days. Little green leaves will sprout up and then the plants will get big. In a few weeks we will be eating a lot of beans, Uncle Robb says."

Uncle Robb stands and straightens up a bit slowly. He is smiling.

"We went to the garden store and bought some plants. Uncle Robb fed the tomato plants and I watered them. Who knew that tomato plants like to eat?" Maria laughs. She gently pats down the soil around the seeds she has planted and stands up. She picks up the hose and aims a spray of water gently onto the row of seeds.

Tara smiles at her uncle. He and her aunt always did the garden together, and he did not seem interested in planting it without her. Looks like he has a new gardening partner.

After dinner the three of them sit on the porch, quietly listening to the last of the bird calls. Uncle Robb stands up slowly.

"Guess I will turn in." He smiles at Maria. "Thanks for your gardening help."

"You're welcome. When Grandma had a garden, we helped her pick vegetables when we visited her."

After Robb goes in, Maria and Tara sit quietly for a while.

"Do you have a boyfriend?" Maria's voice is soft, as if she's not sure she should ask this question.

Tara sighs. "No, not right now."

"Why not?"

"It's complicated."

Maria waits.

"I had a boyfriend, Kyle. We were together for three years. And then it did not work out between us."

"What did not work?"

"We just wanted different things, I guess."

"What did you want?"

"Well, that is the thing. I am not sure. I worked at a job that I liked okay. And when I met Kyle, he seemed like a good guy."

"But he was not? A good guy?" Maria frowns.

"He is. But that was not enough as it turned out. He worked in tech and decided to take a job in Texas."

"You didn't want to go to Texas, too?"

"I didn't want to go just because he went. And in the end, he decided the job was more important than me."

"Oh. He should not have done that." Maria looks worried.

"I thought that at the time. But now, I think he was right. We just did not have enough of a connection to keep us together."

"That's kinda sad."

"Yes, it is. But it's okay. I will be okay."

Maria nods, but still looks concerned.

When Tara gets to her room, she sees a text from her friend Amber.

"Looking at pics from our last trip, Hawaii. Before Covid. Now that we can travel, let's plan something exotic. Portugal? Jamaica? Japan?" She ends with a smiley sun.

Amber works in a hospital lab. During the pandemic, she had to wear a mask all day, every day, which wasn't fun. And working at the hospital was stressful. But her hours were never cut, so her vacation fund is probably larger than Tara's. Tara doesn't think she can afford a vacation anytime soon. For now, she will just enjoy doing what she can in northern Michigan. She texts back to Amber.

"Good idea. Let's talk about it soon."

For now, Tara will travel vicariously through her aunt's journal.

Sixteen

Nice, France
1971

Samedi, 12 Juin

I still have not received a letter from my mom. She usually
writes every week. Is she mad at me for staying in Europe to
travel over the summer?

Miguel and I leave tomorrow to take the train to Paris,
and then we will fly to London. I wrote to my parents once
more and I'll hope for the best, as I will not be able to receive
mail while we are traveling. They will welcome me home
when I do fly back to the States, but I hope they won't be too
upset with me. My sister wrote that she would talk to Mom
and Dad and calm them down.

I told Brian that I am traveling for the summer, but I did
not tell him I would be with Miguel. I have deceived him all
this time because I could not bear to send him a Dear John
letter. I need to talk to him in person, and I am still not sure
what to say. Is it possible to love two people at the same time?
It feels wrong, but I think I do. I should not have let myself
get involved with Miguel. It was not fair to him or to Brian at
home. But it isn't like I set out to make it happen. It just happened! Too confusing.

Monday, June 14

When we arrived in London, the customs officer asked me a
lot of questions about what I would be doing, where I would
stay, how much money I had. I do not have much money left.
We are traveling on the money Miguel gets from his parents
every month. Fortunately, Miguel stepped up and explained.
The officer looked at me and then waved us through.

Anna, whom we met at the Université in Nice, said we
could stay at her family's house for a couple of days. We took
the Metro to the suburb of London where she lives. Riding a
subway was a first for me, as I have never lived where there
were subways. It was weird traveling underground. I felt uneasy, so I wrote this poem.

> The City Tunnel Creature
> Out of the darkness it comes,
> hissing,
> abruptly halting,
> packing small creatures into its stomach.
> It hisses to another stop,
>
> spews out creatures,
> who crawl out of its sides
> into a dimly lighted vein.
> Slowly, listlessly
>
> they inch their way upward
> into the smiling sun,
> which breathes the freshness of air
> back into their world.

Anna's house is in a quiet neighborhood with tree-lined
streets. It is a two-story brick house with a porch across the
front and a large bay window. It has been many months since

I stayed in a real house in a real neighborhood, so I am delighted.

Anna does not have any brothers or sisters, and her dad was not home because he is traveling for his job, so the house seemed very quiet. Her mom welcomed us, and Anna showed us our rooms upstairs, which are very nice. We each have our own room. Mine has a double bed with a flowered bedspread. The large window overlooks the back garden, very peaceful. It's kind of funny that we have separate rooms because we will be traveling together with one small tent. Probably Anna's mom would not approve of us sleeping together.

We are allowed to talk to Anna and her mom while they work in the kitchen, but we cannot touch anything or help prepare the meal or wash the dishes. They keep a kosher kitchen where dishes and work areas are divided between milk and meat. So, they are afraid we will mix things up.

Tuesday, June 15

Anna showed us around her neighborhood and told us what it was like to grow up here. Mostly, she felt comfortable but then started to think about people who didn't have as easy a life as she does. She wants to do something to make the world better.

In the afternoon, she took us out to tea in a beautiful garden café. We sat outside, surrounded by trees and flowers and listened to the birds singing. Anna ordered a traditional English tea with scones, cucumber sandwiches, and tarts. Tea, of course, in elegant porcelain cups. It was very fun, very English.

In the evening after dinner, we sat outside in the backyard. Anna and Miguel discussed what they thought about socialism. Anna stayed on a kibbutz in Israel one summer and really liked it. She thinks she would like to live like that where everyone contributes and shares things.

Miguel thinks there will be revolutions in Latin America to establish socialist governments. He said lots of people there are poor, and he wants to help make their lives better. I did not say much, as I don't know what I think. I definitely want everyone to have what they need and not be poor. Just not sure how to do that.

In the States many college students are protesting the war in Vietnam, but there isn't a lot of talk about socialism among the people that I know. Here in France, I have met students from different places in the world who talk about socialism and making big changes. The 1968 student rebellion in France was not long ago. French students still remember that time and are proud of what they did, even though they did not change things as much as they wanted to.

Wednesday, June 16

We said goodbye to Anna and took the train into London. I loved the National Art Gallery. When my humanities class visited Chicago, the Chicago Art Institute was one of my favorite parts of the trip because I had never been to a large art museum before. Today, I visited another one.

I spent a long time looking at The Sunflowers by Van Gogh because I love flowers, and his impressionist view of them intrigued me. I was curious about Vermeer's Young Woman Standing at a Virginal, both because the painting had a pearly light, and because I wondered about the word in the title, Virginal. Obviously, it was an instrument, but why would it be called that? Miguel didn't know why it was called that either. Kind of strange. Cezanne's painting The Bathers seemed risqué for the late 1800s, all the bathers are naked. Enjoyed the art!

Many students hung out in Trafalgar Square, from all over. Most of them are hitchhiking around England or going on to the Continent to travel around Europe. Everyone was friendly and people played guitars and sang. For lunch we ate at a café and tried steak and kidney pie because it's British. Interesting, but I did not like it much.

We are both fans of Sherlock Holmes, so we found the address that is supposed to be where his office was located. It's not a real address, but you can look through the window and see how it might have looked when Sherlock Holmes worked there. Funny!

We walked by Buckingham Palace. We wanted to see the changing of the guard, just because we have heard about it a lot. But it only happens at certain times during the day, and we had missed it.

For dinner we went to the Great American Disaster. It looked like an American restaurant and played familiar popular American music. People were lined up down the sidewalk, so we had to wait quite a while to get in.

Miguel always starts up conversations, so we chatted with students from France and all over. First American hamburger I have had since January! Very different from what passes for a hamburger in England, where a hamburger tastes more like ham than beef. Given how busy the restaurant was, I guess American hamburgers are popular.

Friday, June 18

Yesterday we visited Hyde Park and listened to people at Speakers Corner for a while. All kinds of people spoke, about religion and politics and art. Small crowds of people gathered to listen to one person and then drifted on to hear someone else. It reminded me of living in the dorm where groups of us talked about these things.

We ate delicious ice cream cones from an ice cream truck. Dairy products in England, like ice cream and cheese, taste rich and creamy. Also, there are some great pastries at the bakeries. We don't have a lot of money, but we splurge now and then.

Today we visited the London Zoo and saw the panda that was loaned to them from China. Lots of people lined up to see him. I felt sorry that people stared at him sitting behind the glass on the front of his enclosure. I would rather see him up a tree in the forest eating bamboo. At least maybe people will want to protect pandas when they see how cute they are.

We walked by Number 10 Downing St. because it is famous, often referred to in books and movies. It wasn't anything special, and we did not see the Prime Minister or anything.

Sunday, June 20

Left London and took the train to Salisbury, hitchhiked part
of the way, and then walked the rest of the way to Stonehenge. I have never seen anything like it. There are two circles
of stones. The outer ones are sarsen stones and the inner ones
are bluestones. It was built 3000 to 2000 BC. The sign said
people think the stones are aligned so that on the summer
solstice you can see the sunrise.

We walked among the stones and tried to imagine what it
was like for people long ago to visit this as a sacred place. Interesting to think about people who lived on earth before us
and built Stonehenge, and we don't really know much about
them.

From Stonehenge we hitchhiked to Plymouth on the English Channel. We stayed in a room in the upstairs of a pub.
There were only a couple of rooms, and we were the only
people staying there.

Monday, June 21

Today we made it to a campground on the coast. It is next to a beautiful, long sandy beach. The guy who runs the campground was very nice. We arrived kind of late because it took us a long time to hitchhike here, and he gave us a couple of pasties from the camp store café because we had not eaten dinner.

We pitched our little tent and laid out our sleeping bags, and then went down to walk along the beach. The ocean was calm, and I stood and gazed out at the vast expanse of it and breathed in the salty tang of the air. There were a few other people on the beach, but it is such a long strip of sand that it was not crowded. I feel happy to be on the beach again, more like what I am used to when I am home in Michigan, sandy, no pebbles.

Tuesday, June 22

Today we spent the day on the beach in the warm sun and swam in the English Channel. It was great to relax for the day. It is really fun to hitchhike from place to place, but it is a bit stressful at times, getting rides and finding places to stay at the end of the day. I'm ready to just relax for a while.

Late afternoon Miguel decided we should swim out to the rocks and collect clams, so we did. He built a fire on a stone ledge along the shore and cooked them. We melted some butter as well, and the clams tasted okay, not a favorite of mine. A young seagull sat on the ledge to join us, and Miguel fed him some clams. The seagull had a big appetite. When we got back to our tent, we were tired and fell asleep pretty early.

Friday, June 25

Yesterday we packed up our small tent, sleeping bags, and cook set and started down the road again. I was sorry to leave the coast because I love the beach and the ocean. But I want to see Wales and Scotland and more of England.

It took us two days to get rides to Cardiff, the capital of Wales. We ate fish and chips from a food stand by the water and again spent the night in a room above a pub. We were surprised when the waitress brought tea up to our room first thing in the morning. Never had that happen anywhere before, but it was a nice way to start the day.

We visited Cardiff Castle which has been standing for 2,000 years. The 12-sided Keep is made of gray stone with a tower entryway. The rooms of the Castle are elaborately decorated. What would it be like to live in a castle like this?

Saturday, June 26

This morning we hitched a ride to Caerphilly Castle. It is not very far from Cardiff. The castle is gloomy and dark with very small windows. We crossed a short drawbridge to walk around the inner part of the castle. I guess not all castles are glamorous, like we usually think they are. They were just places to live that could be defended if attacked. Seems a strange way to live, though, especially feeling the need for defense at all times.

Sunday, June 27

Today we started hitchhiking to the Snowdon Mountains in the north of Wales. There is a national park there where we can camp for a few days and climb the mountain. The names of the towns are in Welsh, and we do not know how to pronounce them because their names have many consonants and few vowels. When someone stops to offer us a ride, we point to the place on the map where we are going. People are good-natured about it, and sometimes they laugh when we try to pronounce the names of the towns.

We walked for a while with a group of cows who were ambling down the road. And stopped to watch two herd dogs round up sheep in a field. The farmer came over and talked with us. He is very proud of his dogs and told us about them. One of the dogs is experienced and is training the younger one. We did not make it to Snowdon, so we just found a place to pitch our tent in the woods along the road.

Tuesday, June 29

Yesterday we got a ride to Snowdon Park and set up our camp. The ranger let us put up our tent in the area where we can build a fire, because we don't have a stove to cook on. We were tired, so we are relaxing today and checking out the area. We walked down the road just outside the park. Walls built of stacks of old and weathered stones lined the sides of the road.

We can see the mountains from our campsite. Although it looks like a long climb, I look forward to reaching the top and seeing the view in all directions. Miguel cooked our dinner over a fire that he built with wood he found in the park. Our tent is very small, but cozy.

Tara stops reading. It seems that her aunt was pretty serious about Miguel. She must have felt confused to love both him and Brian. Tara does not think she has ever felt strongly about two men at the same time. She loved Kyle, at first anyway, and one love was enough for her.

She is surprised that Aunt Becca knew people who talked about socialism, as she had never thought of her aunt as a leftist. Aunt Becca was progressive, though, always defending people's civil rights.

Funny that the Great American Disaster was a popular novelty in 1971, because now McDonald's seems to be everywhere.

Speakers' Corner sounds interesting. A place set up where people could orate or opine would give lots of people the chance to spout off about whatever issues they care about. She wonders if that still happens in London.

People were really into the Chinese panda. Tara wonders how the panda felt about it. Maybe his sojourn at the zoo helped to mobilize people to care more about preserving wildlife. Still seems sad to see him behind a glass window and not in the wild where he belongs.

In some ways people are now more aware of how quickly plants and animals can become extinct. Yet, it's still happening, especially with climate change, and Tara worries the world is not doing enough to stop it.

Seventeen

Summer 2023

Tara stops at the food co-op on her way home from work. Three people require a lot more food than two people do, but she is glad that Uncle Robb and Maria are both eating. Although a couple of nights ago at dinner, Maria announced that she decided to become a vegetarian.

"Why do you want to be a vegetarian?" Robb looked puzzled. "I know more people are choosing that these days, but won't you miss meat?"

"No, there are lots of other things to eat, and it's better for the planet. Cows emit a lot of methane which contributes to climate change."

"That's true." Tara takes climate change seriously, so Maria's decision makes some sense to her. "We will have to experiment and see what we like."

"Jayden is a vegetarian, well pescatarian anyway, and his mom fixes dinner for him. You could ask her."

"Good idea. So, how was your day?" She looked at both of them, wanting to change the subject. Tara's friend Melanie was a vegetarian and cooked really great food, so it could not be too hard. That night Tara searched the internet to find palatable recipes. Mexican meals seemed like a good option because they please both vegetarians and meat eaters.

The house is quiet. She puts away the groceries and goes into the backyard where Uncle Robb pulls weeds from the garden. He looks up and waves, and she waves back.

Under the large maple tree along the back fence, she notices the hammock set up under the tree. One leg draped over the side, Maria gently rocks the hammock back and forth, back and forth.

"Hola, Maria. Qué pasa?" Tara remembers some beginning Spanish and is pleased with herself. Maria looks up.

"What are you reading?"

Maria holds up the book to show her the cover. It looks like some kind of fantasy story, with a scary-looking dragon and a heroic-looking character on the front.

"Don't know that book."

Maria gives her a shrug as if to say of course someone her age would not know the book.

"Jayden brought it over. He usually reads on his notepad, but his sister bought him this book because she says reading a real book is better. Anyway, Jayden saw I was almost finished with the first book, and he had just finished the second one, this one. The third book of the trilogy won't come out until next year."

"Nice of Jayden." Tara smiles.

Maria smiles and goes back to reading.

When they are eating dinner Maria asks, "Uncle Robb, what did you do before you retired?"

Uncle Robb looks surprised. "I worked with a former professor entering data for his research. He discovered I was good with computers and suggested I take a computer programming course. I did that and then worked at the U a few years. When Rebecca and I moved up north, I set up computers for companies, got into website design, taught at the community college."

"Did you like doing that?"

"I did. I felt like I was helping people with something they didn't know how to do."

"Jayden says when I go to high school in the fall, I should take web design."

"Probably a good idea. Everyone has to have a website."

"I guess so."

"But you should take classes for what you're interested in doing, as much as you can."

"I'm not sure what that is."

"You have to try things out. It takes time. And it can change when you get to college, even as you get older."

Maria nods.

Tara watches the discussion, surprised to hear how grown-up Maria sounds. And pleased that Maria trusts Uncle Robb's opinion. The two of them seem to be getting along well. She feels relieved. Maybe she is not responsible for making sure everyone is happy. Maybe they can find their way without her. Does she take responsibility for others so she doesn't have to find her own way?

"I'll do the dishes." Maria stacks plates and silverware and carries them to the sink.

"I'll dry them." Uncle Robb starts clearing the table. He looks at Tara. "You go on and relax for a while."

Tara hesitates. "Thanks." She sits on the back porch with her phone, intending to respond to a couple of friends who texted her. She holds the phone in her hand and looks out on the garden. Vegetables are beginning to appear on the plants, and the flowers in her aunt's garden bloom, weed-free.

What does she want for herself? These days with her uncle are peaceful and Maria is doing well, but she feels restless. She is comfortable working at the toy store, but that is not what she wants to do long-term. One of the things that is most important to her is the natural environment. She cherishes the knowledge she acquired from her aunt and thinks she might pursue that.

After the dishes, Uncle Robb sits in his chair beside her, while Maria goes to her room to call her mom and sister.

"So, what do you think? Maria seems settled." Uncle Robb rocks his chair back and forth.

Tara nods. "She seems happy here and has made friends, found her voice."

"What about you? Thoughts about what you will do at the end of the summer?"

Her uncle seems to have read her mind. "Thinking about it. Since I've been here, I realize how much I learned about nature from you and Aunt Becca. Maybe there is some way I can use that."

He smiles. "Glad you learned something useful from us. Sounds like the start of a plan."

Later in her room, Tara takes out her aunt's journal. Where are she and Miguel in their travels now? How did her aunt get from her experience in France and a relationship with Miguel to a successful and long life with Uncle Robb?

Eighteen

Wales
1971

Friday, July 2

Yesterday, we climbed a peak in the Snowdon Mountains. Mt Snowdown is the highest mountain in Wales, Yr Wyddfa in Welsh, and Edmund Hilary climbed part of it to train before he climbed Mt. Everest. The park ranger told us it is also the burial place of Rhita Gawr, the strongest of all the giants that were vanquished by King Arthur. So, I felt like we were doing something very adventurous.

It took a few hours because it's a pretty steep climb. I only brought sandals to walk in, which didn't work out very well because my feet sometimes slipped on the rocks. We made it to the top, though, and it was really exciting. We could look in all directions at the other mountain peaks, many blue-grey lakes, and stark green plains. The sky was sunny and brilliant blue, but fog hung over some of the peaks in the distance.

The hike down was a bit easier, but I slipped on a stone and fell. I don't know why, but I started to cry. My ankle hurt, but it wasn't the pain that made me cry. I just suddenly felt homesick and wanted to go home. At first Miguel thought I had really hurt myself, but when I said I was homesick, he just looked at me. He helped me stand up, and I limped back down the mountain.

Back at our tent, we were too tired to cook anything, so we ate sandwiches and canned fruit for dinner. I did not even write in my journal. I am a little worried because Miguel didn't seem as sympathetic as I wish he had. I think maybe he felt hurt that I am not happy enough being with him. Neither of us said much about it, though. Has he stopped caring about me? Are we spending too much time together? Will we stay together when it's time for me to go home?

We decided to stay here another day before we hitchhike to Liverpool, so I can rest my feet. Miguel went for a walk, but I stayed near camp and read mostly. Miguel and I were kind to each other, but careful. Things do not feel okay between us.

Saturday, July 3

It took us a while to get a ride from the park, but hitchhiking across northern Wales was pretty easy. It still hurts to walk, but I tried to act like it didn't. Miguel asked how I was, but didn't seem to notice that I sometimes limped. We ran out of water, and Miguel actually knocked on the door of a house in a small town and asked the woman who answered if we could fill our canteens. I thought maybe people wouldn't like that, but the woman was friendly and filled our canteens for us. She asked us where we were from and where we were going.

On the other side of the town, a van picked us up with five people about our age, three girls and two boys. They were nice, but one girl started picking lice out of another girl's head, and I almost freaked out! I was really glad when they got where they were going and let us out of the van. I do not want to get lice! Especially while we are traveling! I kept itching my head for the rest of the day.

We made it to just south of Liverpool and found a place to camp for the night.

Sunday, July 4

We walked around Liverpool, home of the Beatles and all. We found Penny Lane and the barbershop that is mentioned in the song. We stood outside the Cavern Club where the Beatles first played (before Ringo joined them). And also, Queen, and one of my favorites, Gerry and the Pacemakers.

What I really wanted to do was cross the Mersey, in honor of the song, "Ferry Cross the Mersey." In high school Brian and I listened to Gerry and the Pacemakers. I always wondered about the Mersey in the song. It's just a river, of course. The ferry has crossed the river for centuries, since the Benedictine monks ran the first service in 1515. But now the service is limited, so I didn't get to cross the Mersey. I was disappointed.

Funny. Today t is the Fourth of July back in the States. But here it is not celebrated because the British lost their colony back then. It feels weird that the U.S. was a British colony. The Brits we meet don't seem that much different from us. Different culture in lots of ways but just people, like us.

Monday, July 5

We got a ride to Glasgow and walked through the city. Glasgow seems to be an industrial city, and we didn't see anything very interesting. Maybe we just didn't take the time because we are in a hurry to get to Loch Ness.

Then we hitched a ride headed for Inverness to see Nessie, but Loch Ness is very far north and we had trouble getting rides, so we had to find a place to stay until tomorrow. Miguel is never afraid to ask someone for something.

We stopped at a nice house with a yard and he asked if we could pitch our tent in their yard for the night. The woman who answered the door seemed hesitant, but finally said we could. When her husband got home, he invited us in and asked us to stay for supper. He is Irish and his wife is Scottish. Then their daughter came home from work, and they were all friendly and asked us a lot of questions. They said we could stay in the spare bedroom instead of camping in the yard. That was so nice of them! And it was wonderful to sleep in a bed!

The next morning, the parents had both gone to work when we got up. The daughter fixed us breakfast and said her mother wanted her to drive us into town so we could go to a bank and get money to pay for our room and breakfast. We were surprised because no one had said anything about that, but it seemed fair enough as we had gotten a nice place to stay and a delicious hot meal. When we were driving into town, the three of us talked a lot. She wanted to know all about us, and we were interested to hear about her life in Scotland.

Wednesday, July 7

Yesterday we got some short rides and walked quite a lot. We saw Loch Lomond and sang the song about it. Today we finally got a long ride from a truck driver who took us to Inverness where the Loch Ness visitor center is located.

I was surprised to see castles, because the States doesn't have castles like that just sitting around. There are lots of lochs, and finally we saw Loch Ness and the ruins of Urquhart Castle. The truck driver pointed the castle out and told us about it. King Macbethad had a castle in Inverness, and Shakespeare based the character of Macbeth on him. We also saw lots of Scottish cows. They are big, brown, and very shaggy, not like Michigan cows.

Thursday, July 8

The Loch Ness Centre and Exhibit is built along the shore of Loch Ness, the second-deepest lake in Scotland and the largest after Loch Lomond. Nessie has supposedly been spotted in the Loch many times. She is supposed to be a long, snakelike creature. Very long.

There are a lot of pictures that have been taken over the years, since about 1933, I think. Some of the pictures do look like there is a creature out there in the loch. More than one picture was blurry, but I could make out a definite line of humps, like a long snake in the water.

One theory is that there was a creature swimming around when this area was still an ocean, and it got trapped when the lake was formed. I think it would be pretty cool if there really was an ancient creature swimming around in the Loch. I wonder if people ever go swimming in the lake. What would Nessie do if she encountered a person?

Monday, July 12

It took us two days to hitchhike from Inverness to Edinburgh. We didn't think we would get a ride overnight, so I got brave and knocked on the door of a farmhouse. When the farm wife answered, I asked if we could pitch our tent in the field by their house. She smiled at me and said we could camp in the backyard, and she would fix our breakfast for a small fee. We slept in the backyard with some chickens stalking around our tent. Breakfast was a real farm breakfast with fresh eggs and milk and homemade bread. We paid her and headed down the road.

Yesterday we made it to the University of Edinburgh late morning. Miguel heard from a Scottish student in Nice that people could rent dorm rooms at the U during the summer. So, we rented a room with a single bed and also got tickets to eat in the cafeteria. Beds, showers and breakfast. A luxury!

The University was established in 1582 and the old part is beautiful. Some of the buildings are newer, of course, and I don't think those are as interesting. Info about the U said the Edinburgh Seven were the first women to graduate from any university in the United Kingdom. And this is the place that inspired Sir Arthur Conan Doyle to create Sherlock Holmes.

We visited the Medieval Old Town and Edinburgh Castle where the Scotland crown jewels are kept and the Stone of Destiny that is used in Scottish coronations. Tomorrow we are going to see Arthur's Seat in Holyrood Park. Edinburgh is a beautiful city.

We are more relaxed with each other. Life is much easier in a room with a bed, showers every day, and breakfast available. Maybe we could make our relationship last. Mostly, I just think about one day at a time. Our travels will not last forever, and I don't know what will happen after that.

Friday, July 16

I was sorry to leave Edinburgh. The dorm rooms were comfortable, and I really like the city.

It took two days to hitchhike to York, which is also a cool city. It was originally a Roman walled city on the Ouse River. There are beautiful cathedrals and what Miguel most wanted to see, the National Railway Museum. He loves trains, especially older ones. So, he was pretty excited to see so many of them. Trains are okay, but I hadn't spent much time on them before coming to Europe, and to me they are just an efficient mode of transportation.

We tend to see whatever Miguel wants to see. But that isn't really his fault. I just don't know as much about the places we are visiting, so it is all interesting to me. I realize that I always let him plan what we will do on our travels. Maybe that isn't so strange given how I was taught that a girl should not call a boy, but wait for him to call her. She cannot ask him out on a date, but must wait for him to make the first move. If you don't follow the rules, boys will think you are "fast" and no one will want to marry you.

Of course, now I think that is all ridiculous, but it's hard to know what to do sometimes. Miguel always seems so sure about what he wants, and I am still trying to figure out so many things. Sometimes I think Miguel is just too worldly and sophisticated for us to be a couple. Life is so complicated!

After reading Aunt Rebecca's journal, Tara lies on her bed and looks out the window. Her aunt climbed a mountain in sandals because that was what she had. Tara and her friends are careful to have the right gear, the right hiking shoes, when they do things like that.

How fun to see pictures of "Nessie." And all the castles, which are just a regular part of the scenery. The U.S. doesn't have castles like that. There is a different kind of history here. Some elaborate societies, like the Aztecs, Incas, and Mayas had temples and big mounds, but not castles.

At this point in her journey, Aunt Becca sounds uncertain if she and Miguel can make their relationship last. But she still seems hopeful. Yet, she lets Miguel make a lot of decisions for her. Tara can't imagine her aunt ever doing that. Aunt Becca always seemed to have definite positions and ideas of her own, although she was willing to listen to what other people said.

She remembers back to when she and Kyle met. It was fun at first, that getting to know someone new. Finding out what he liked, what he liked to do, who his friends were. But then she remembers how he often spent evenings on his computer when she would have liked to go out and do something. And then they started arguing, nothing serious, and they made up afterward. But that was a clue, she thinks now. After the getting to know you part, they didn't seem to have that much in common.

She thinks about her conversation with Maria. That was the first time she had really admitted to herself that Kyle had made the right decision. Their relationship wasn't really going anywhere, and they both needed to move on. She still feels lonely, misses having someone she is close to, to share her life with. But she hopes Kyle is happy in Texas. And if she doesn't find someone else, she will make a life for herself anyway.

Nineteen

Summer 2023

Tara pushes the hammock back and forth, an abandoned book beside her. The sun caresses her face as the hammock sways. Suddenly, the sun winks out and she looks up.

"Ian! What are you doing here?" The hammock bounces as she sits up. She jumps up and hugs him. Then she notices a man standing just behind him. "Oh, hi." She looks at Ian and raises her eyebrows. He smiles.

"Hey, Tara. This is Jonathan."

Jonathan smiles. "Hey, Tara. I've heard so much about you. Great to meet you."

"You, too." Tara laughs. "Although I haven't heard as much about you."

"Yeah. Sorry to surprise you. Jonathan and I have been together for a while, but I did not want to say anything at first. You know, didn't want to jinx it."

"You are both welcome, of course. But I did not know you were coming. Did you visit my mom and your dad?" Tara winces. She never felt comfortable calling her stepdad, dad, because she has her own dad. She shrugs because she knows she doesn't have to explain to Ian.

"No worries." Ian nudges her playfully. "We did visit them."

"And?" She always thought Ian moved to Seattle to get away from the family.

"Your mom was okay with it. She was not surprised."

"Yeah, Mom usually figures things out and then waits to be told about it." She hesitates. "And your dad?"

"It was awkward." He looks at Jonathan.

Jonathan laughs. "That's one way to put it. I can't say I felt welcome exactly, but he didn't say anything weird or mean, just kept kind of quiet and gave me weird looks. Like this." Johnathan crinkles his forehead and his face looks puzzled, but also stern.

"That doesn't look especially friendly. I guess he was surprised? Was Jordan there?"

"Mom called him and he came over for dinner. He seemed okay about it, not overly supportive, but not negative."

"Well, that doesn't sound too bad. A bit awkward, though. Sorry."

"It could have been worse. I was relieved to get it over with."

"Me, too." Jonathan takes a deep breath.

"Well, I'm glad you're here. How long can you stay?"

"Just a couple of nights." Ian laughs. "The look on your face. We got a B and B not too far from here. Jon has to be back at work in a couple of days. Busy time for him right now."

Tara punches him gently on the arm. "We would be happy to have you stay. I was just trying to figure out where we would put you."

"No worries. We met a couple of guys in Detroit who said there are some gay pride things happening up here this week."

"I see. You plan to party."

"Might do a bit of that."

"What do you do? Besides party up north with Ian?" Tara smiles at Jonathan.

"Website design mostly. We have a couple of independent companies who are just getting off the ground, so it's a big rush."

"You and Uncle Robb will get on well, then. He got into web design a few years ago. Did you meet him already?"

"Knocked on the front door, but no one answered. Saw your car in the driveway, so we came back here to see if anyone was around."

"He and Maria must be out. Probably the garden store." Tara gestured toward the garden. "Always something needed."

"Who's Maria? Uncle Robb does not have a new girlfriend already." Ian frowns. "Not that I'd begrudge him that, but it seems a bit sudden, doesn't it?"

Tara laughs. She could not imagine Uncle Robb with anyone but her aunt. "No, no, nothing like that. It's a long story. Let's go get something to drink and I will tell you about it."

They grab drinks and sit on the porch. Tara is in the middle of Maria's story when she hears car doors slam and Maria's excited voice. She and Uncle Robb come around to the backyard, each carrying a couple of plants.

"Ian, what are you doing here?" Uncle Robb sets down the plants he carries, wipes his hands on his shorts, and comes over to give Ian a hug. "Great to see you." He gestures to Jonathan. "You brought a friend."

Ian hugs Uncle Robb and then puts his arm around Jonathan. "This is Jonathan. We were visiting my parents and decided to come up and see how you guys are doing."

Uncle Robb shakes Jonathan's hand. "Great to meet you. Ian and his friends are always welcome. You staying for dinner?"

"Sure, if that's okay."

"We would love to have you stay. I'd like to hear what you have been up to out there in Oregon." Uncle Robb raises an eyebrow and Ian and Jonathan both laugh.

"Jonathan is a website artist."

"Something like that. I like to think I'm using some artistic skills."

"I am not as artistic as I would like to be." Uncle Robb shakes his head. "Tell me more about what you do."

Tara sits and listens, happy to have Ian and his boyfriend here. Ian's face glows with pride while he watches Jonathan talk to Uncle Robb, and Tara is very happy for him. She pushes away the thought that she wants what he has.

Ian gestures with his head, always the signal between them when they were growing up that one of them needed to talk. Tara follows him out to the front porch.

"So, how are you really? I know how close you and Aunt Becca were."

"I'm sad. Now it's off and on, not a steady sadness like in the beginning. Sometimes I don't think about it, but often something reminds me of her, and I feel cheated out of more time with her."

"Sorry. Grief is hard. Your aunt was great, always took time to make me feel part of the family. I always felt she knew I was gay, and she encouraged me just to be myself."

"She was like that."

"So, new boyfriend? Plans for the future? What are you doing with yourself up here?"

"No boyfriend, taking a break. Thinking about the future. Looking out for Uncle Robb and Maria."

"Good enough. It'll come to you. Speaking of that, I have three tickets to see the Accidentals tonight at a concert at the Opera House. I remembered you liked their music, and we thought it would be cool to see the old opera house."

"I don't know if I'm ready for going out."

"Of course, you're ready. You need to get back out there and enjoy life more. Besides, it will be fun. You will be with Jonathan and me. What could be more entertaining?"

Tara laughs. "Good point. You win. I'll have to change my clothes, though."

"We'll wait."

The three of them walk downtown, Ian telling Tara all about Oregon and what she might do out there.

"You make a good case for visiting you."

"Good. That is the plan."

A crowd of people mills about inside the Opera House, and the three of them look at the local art displayed on the walls while they wait to take their seats. A warm-up band of two young men and two women play a lively set, but Tara thinks at one point that one of the players is out of tune.

After the band setup is quickly adjusted by a two-person crew, the Accidentals come on stage to enthusiastic applause and immediately launch into their opening number.

Tara smiles at Ian and turns her full attention to the music that begins to vibrate within her, lifting her spirits. The talent of the three women on stage enthralls her. At the end of the concert, everyone jumps to their feet and cheers wildly.

Outside, Tara puts her arm around Ian and gives him a big hug.

He grins. "Not bad, huh?"

"You were right." She grins back. "Of course."

Ian and Jonathan laugh.

"Don't tell him that. He will get full of himself." Jonathan punches Ian playfully on the arm.

At Uncle Robb's house Ian and Jonathan say goodbye and head off for a late night of partying. Tara feels wistful about not going off to party with a partner.

"Stop by tomorrow before you leave?" Tara calls out.

"Will do. And please come out to Oregon and stay with us for a while." Ian calls back and waves.

"I would love that. I will."

Tara stops by Maria's bedroom to say good night.

"Can I ask you something?"

"Course." Tara hopes this isn't something too serious.

"Are Ian and Jonathan together? You know, together-together."

"Yes, they are."

"That's good. They seem happy together."

"They do. Good night."

Tara sits on her bed and watches a flock of starlings chittering in the trees. Maybe she should go to Oregon at the end of the summer. She would have a place to stay, and maybe she would find what she is looking for out there, possibilities.

What is she looking for? She thought she had found it with Kyle. But maybe she didn't. Perhaps she was looking for stability, security, sameness because her growing-up years had seemed so fragmented, and she often felt unsure of how she fit in. Maybe stability isn't all she is looking for.

She takes out the journals, a trip into someone else's life. Her aunt's summer travels are coming to an end. What will happen when she comes home? Did she find the right person in Miguel? Or was Brian the right one? Or neither. After all, she met Uncle Robb and he seemed just right.

Twenty

York, England
1971

Saturday, July 17

We walked all over York today. After dinner, as we stood by the river, Miguel asked me if I could graduate in one semester instead of two, so I could come back to France sooner. He said it would take him at least a year to finish up his graduate work in France. Maybe I could go home for a short visit and then come back.

I didn't know what to say. I have assumed I would come back to be with Miguel. I also assumed that I was going home to stay. I told Miguel I could check into my credits and see about that when I got back to my university.

Then he started talking about our life together in the future: me coming back to France while he finished his degree (he did not say what I would do during that time), him getting a job as a university professor somewhere and us moving there, somewhere in Latin America.

I just listened. I don't know what to think. That does not sound like my life. He seemed to take my silence as agreement, and we kept on walking. We will soon be back in London, and then I will fly home. I don't know what happens after that. I hate how I can't make up my mind.

Tuesday, July 20

We wanted to take the train to Ipswich, one of the oldest cities in England. But we didn't have enough money and might need it for something later. So, we hitchhiked again. And it took two days to get here.

Ipswich is on the River Orwell (like the author?) It was set up as a port city in the 600s and taken over by the Vikings in the 800s. Ipswich merchants are mentioned in the Canterbury Tales, and Chaucer's family came from here.

We visited the Victoria Natural History Gallery. Miguel wanted to see the insect collection. I said no thanks to that. I'm not a big fan of insects, except for bumblebees and butterflies, but the architecture was beautiful, and the stuffed animals were interesting. I don't really care for killing and stuffing animals, so I kind of didn't like that part.

Saturday, July 31

We camped out at a park east of London for a couple of days before going back to London. To give us some time to relax. I'm not sure that was a good thing, because we both had too much time to think about the fact that this trip is almost over. And what happens with us then?

We talked about it, but Miguel was frustrated that I haven't made up my mind, that I can't give him a definite answer. I still have doubts. I need time to think about it, consider what my decision will mean for my life. We did not come to any conclusion and have stopped talking about it. I didn't even write in my journal because it felt too hard.

Now we are back in London for a couple of days. We wanted to make sure we were here to catch my flight home.

Sunday, August 1

We went to Trafalgar Square today to hang out for the day before I fly back to the States. We were surprised to see hundreds of people protesting. A young man handed us a flyer: "Stop Genocide, Recognize Bangla Desh Rally." People chanted both in English and another language, Bangla someone told us.

Miguel asked the guy with the flyers what the protest was all about. He told us the Bengalis have been fighting for their independence. Pakistan was split into East Pakistan and West Pakistan. Both parts are mostly Muslim, but East Pakistan is culturally different with a different language.

West Pakistan, with arms shipments from the U.S., is attacking East Pakistan, killing and raping as they go. "This is genocide of the Bengalis," the guy said. We nodded, and I said I was sorry that the U.S. supported this. I thought to myself, isn't killing people in Vietnam enough for our military?

So, we stayed at the protest for a while, and we were among the few white people there. We felt welcome, though. Why is the world so crazy with people killing and raping other people?

Miguel and I felt a bit demoralized at the end of our trip. We had not kept up with the news, as we had been traveling. Traveling and just thinking about where we were going was a nice break from all the terrible things that can happen in the world.

We met a student from England who supports the Bengalis. He told us that George Harrison had organized the Concert for Bangladesh at Madison Square Garden that is happening today. He told us all the singers and bands that are performing. Wish we could have been there!

Monday, August 2

Tonight, we are spending the night in the London airport as we will both fly out tomorrow and we have run out of money to pay for a hotel room. Miguel has fallen asleep, slumped over to the side in his chair. A lot of young people are waiting in the airport overnight. The air in the terminal smells stale with many bodies and the leftover aromas of food.

I am really tired after traveling and hanging out in London today, but I cannot sleep. I have not said anything to Miguel, but I don't know if we will ever see each other again. This trip together has been fun in a lot of ways, but it is clear that we are very different, and that has caused us to argue a lot when we spend so much time together. In Nice we were almost never alone together.

The last few days Miguel has repeated several times that I must learn Spanish so that when he finishes his program next year and we go back to Latin America, I will be able to speak the language. But we have not decided together that we will go back to Latin America.

I don't think I can go that far from my family and friends and everything I know. I wish I were more adventuresome, but although I have loved my time in Europe, I am ready to go home. I miss my parents and my sister and my dog and cat. I miss my friends and all the things in my life that are familiar.

I miss Brian, although I don't know if he still is my Brian or not. The song "The Long and Winding Road" keeps coming to mind. I still care about him. Can someone love two people at the same time? It seems so, but that can't work out.

I decided to just say goodbye and leave things open when I walk away from Miguel to get on the plane back to America. Maybe things will work out for us. We will write and see what comes of that. I am sad and confused.

Tara wonders what happened with East and West Pakistan. Why did the U.S. support one side that was killing the other? She opens her laptop and looks up the Concert for Bangladesh. Of the featured musicians, she is familiar with George Harrison and Ringo Starr, of course. And Bob Dylan and Eric Clapton. She doesn't think she has heard of Billy Preston, Leon Russell, or Badfinger. Why were there not any women musicians featured? Famous women like Joni Mitchell, Judy Collins, Joan Baez.

Miguel seems serious about Aunt Becca going back to France to be with him. He does not seem to have doubts. What happened when her aunt came home? Did they decide to end their communication or did it just slide away? Did Aunt Rebecca regret the end of the relationship? Or was she relieved? Did she ever think about what might have been?

Tara is sure that her aunt really loved her uncle. They seemed like such a great fit. But she seemed to love Miguel, too. And there was Brian whom she left here in the States when she went to France. What happened to him? Was Aunt Rebecca sad? Was he sad?

She had just read the last entry. She wanted the story to continue. Too many unanswered questions to which she would like to know the answers. But one thing is for sure. She is glad Aunt Becca married Uncle Robb and stayed in the U.S.

There are some empty pages that she wishes had been filled. When she closes the journal, she feels something stuffed in the back of it. Turning the last empty page, she discovers a few letters to her aunt from Miguel. She is eager to read them, but begIns to yawn. Tomorrow. What will the letters say? Did Aunt Becca answer them?

Twenty-one

September 1971

Rebecca sat on the front porch of her apartment building, resting her head on her hand, and watched the cars on the street. Leaves on the maple trees waved gently in the mild fall breeze. A few students walked by on their way home from Friday classes. Talking non-stop, they did not notice Rebecca.

The weekend stretched out ahead of her. Two of her roommates had gone home, and a third was already working on a paper in the library. If things were normal, Brian would be coming to visit her for the weekend. But it felt like nothing would ever be normal again. She brushed tears from her eyes.

"Hello? Everything okay?"

She looked up. A tall, angular young man with wavy brown hair stood on the sidewalk. He looked at her with concern. Rebecca hesitated. She felt like an idiot sitting on the porch, crying.

"I'm fine."

"You all alone?"

Rebecca looked at him closely. That sounded like trouble. But he looked so sincere. "Not exactly. My roommate will be home soon."

"My name is Robb. What's yours?"

"Rebecca."

"I live just down the street. On my way home from a class. Mind if I sit down for a few minutes?"

Rebecca shrugged. She did not want to be alone, and he seemed harmless enough.

Robb walked slowly over to the porch and sat down a couple of feet from her.

"Don't mean to bother you, but you look sad, and I could not just walk on by." He looked at her.

"That was kind of you. It's nothing really. Normally, Brian, my boyfriend, would be coming to visit."

"He couldn't come?" A boyfriend, huh?

"We broke up."

Robb stopped himself from smiling. "Sorry to hear that. Breakups are tough. Your idea or his or both?"

"Mostly his, I guess. But he's right. Since I got home from France, I'm not the same as I was before I left."

"You were in France? How long?"

"Six months, and then I traveled through England, Scotland, and Wales for a couple of months."

"Not surprising you would not be the same, then. Do you want to be? The same, I mean?"

Rebecca smiled a little. "That's a good question. I would not change all that I learned by going there. But it would be easier if I hadn't gone."

"Learning is usually a good thing."

"That's true. Anyway, that's how it turned out. Maybe we were not meant to stay together anyway. Hard to tell."

"Did he find someone else while you were gone, do you think?"

"I don't think so." Rebecca is quiet.

"Did you find someone else?"

"Maybe. I don't know. Anyway, what about you? How's your love life?"

Robb laughed. "That's a good question, too. I've been dating this woman for a few weeks, but we're both graduating and I'm not sure what will happen then. I don't think either of us is ready for a big commitment."

"Same here. Graduating. And that feels like jumping off into a void. I don't have a job yet. And I'm not sure what I want to do."

"That's a common theme. My roommates are all pretty uncertain about what they're going to do. And so am I. Should I go on to grad school? Not sure I'm ready or if I even want to do that."

"Same here."

Robb looked at his watch. "Looks like it's time for dinner. There's that new, natural foods restaurant at the end of the street. Want to continue our conversation there?"

"Okay. Let me get my jacket. In case it gets cool later." Rebecca went inside, came back out, and locked the apartment door.

They walked down the street, passing other students ready to enjoy a Friday night. Tall, expansive trees shaded the street, their leaves taking on just a tinge of fall color. The setting sun cast a golden glow that filtered through the trees.

"What's your degree in?" Rebecca looked up at Robb.

"Math and economics."

"What will you do with that, do you think? What kind of job might you get?"

"That's a good question. It seemed like a good idea at the time, but now it doesn't seem so easy."

"I know what you mean. I'm getting a degree teaching social studies and English. It's supposed to get me a job. But I don't even think I want to teach. Next semester I'm supposed to student teach, but should I bother?"

"Another good question."

They walked on in silence. The street ended at a bigger street that led to the downtown. They stopped on the corner beside a rectangular, old brick, two-story building. A sign on the entrance to a business on the first floor said, "Lost Wax Candles." They followed another couple up the stairs on the side of the building to the restaurant on the second floor, "Just Food."

The door opened into a room with walls of weathered wood. Simple wooden tables and chairs were lined up by the windows along the front of the building and along the side walls. They read the sign, "Seat yourself." Next to the sign the menu was printed on a blackboard: green salad, potato soup, vegetable soup, vegetables with brown rice, lentils with brown rice, and pinto beans with brown rice. Drinks included herbal teas and coffee.

Robb nodded toward a table in the corner beside a window and gave her a questioning look. She nodded back and followed him there. A waitress in bell-bottom jeans and a colorful embroidered shirt came to their table and asked for their order. "I'll have the salad and vegetables with rice." She looked at Robb.

"I'll try the vegetable soup and the pinto beans with rice."

"To drink?"

"Mint tea," they said at the same time.

"Where does your family live? Parents? Siblings?" Robb leaned back in his chair and looked at Rebecca.

"Up north. I have parents." She laughed. "And one sister, younger than me. How about you?"

"I have two parents as well." He laughed. "One brother. My parents live in a suburb of Detroit, and my older brother works in Chicago."

The waitress brought their food, and they ate silently, suddenly feeling shy. After all, they had only just met. They sipped their tea.

"When you were a child, what did you want to be when you grew up?" Rebecca set down her mug of tea and looked over at Robb.

"Like many little boys, I wanted to be a policeman. Our teacher put up posters on the bulletin board of a friendly man in a blue uniform helping a child. He had a nice smile on his face, and the child looked happy. Needless to say, these days being a cop does not sound very promising. Busting heads at demonstrations and such."

"I had not thought about those posters for a while. We were told, if you are in trouble, ask a policeman for help. I would not do that now, though."

"What about you? What did you want to be?"

"I wanted to work in a zoo, taking care of animals. But now I'm not sure I even think zoos are a good idea."

"Life is complicated."

When they were ready to leave, Robb picked up her jacket from the back of the chair and handed it to her. Their hands touched and they each felt a frisson of connection.

Robb walked her home. When they reached Rebecca's apartment building, they looked at each other and smiled.

"Thanks. You rescued me, at least for now. That was very kind of you." She hesitated, feeling like he should kiss her but they hardly knew each other.

"My pleasure." Robb could not think of what to say. He didn't want this to be the end, but he was afraid to push. What if she said no thanks? "I could give you a call, maybe. If I had your phone number."

"Okay."

He pulled out a pen from his pocket and held up his hand. "What's the number?"

Rebecca laughed and wrote her number on the back of his hand. She is reluctant to let go of his hand.

"Have a good summer."

"You, too." Rebecca opened her apartment door, waved, and watched him walk away down the street, wondering if she should have done something differently.

Robb walked home, annoyed with himself. Should he have said something more, done something more?

Twenty-two

Summer 2023

Maria stands in the doorway of the living room. Uncle Robb looks up from his book.

"Is it lunchtime? I can make you a sandwich."

"No, thank you. It's only 11:00."

Uncle Robb waits. "Something else?"

Maria takes a breath. "I saw a couple of boats in the garage. Hanging from the ceiling."

"Oh, those are kayaks. We used to take them out a lot. On the small lakes near here."

Maria notices that he does not say Rebecca's name. She knows that saying her name often brings tears to Uncle Robb's eyes.

"Was it fun? I've never been in a boat before."

"It was a lot of fun." Uncle Robb looks at Maria. "We could take them out, I guess."

Maria nods. "I can swim only a little."

"There are life vests, and we can stay close to shore." Uncle Robb gets up from the chair. "Guess I should go and start getting things ready. No time like the present."

Maria follows him to the garage and watches Uncle Robb lower the kayaks to the garage floor and unhook them. Maria helps him carry them out to the pickup truck and heft them into the back. Uncle Robb climbs in, hooks each kayak to a tie-down ring in the truck bed, and jumps out.

"Grab those two paddles." He points at the paddles on a shelf along the wall. He pulls a container off the shelf and loads it into the back. Maria slides the paddles in next to the container.

"That takes care of the gear we need. Let's get us some water and maybe snacks."

"What about Taffy? Does she like to ride in the boat? Can she go, too?"

"Taffy is a great kayaker. And she loves to take a swim in the water when she's done."

On the drive to the lake, they pass cherry orchards and a farm with cows standing by a small pond. Uncle Robb turns down a gravel road and the truck bumps over the potholes. He looks at Maria.

"You okay? Not afraid of water, are you?"

Maria shakes her head. "I don't think so. We used to swim in a pool sometimes. At the water park. It had a wave pool and a slide."

"Well, this is a bit different. I think you'll like it. This lake is quiet, peaceful. Might see an egret or some loons."

"Oh." Maria knows that an egret is a large white bird, but isn't sure what a loon looks like.

Uncle Robb turns the truck onto a dirt road and drives down a small hill into the parking lot. There is one other car and Maria spots a rowboat out in the middle of the lake.

"Looks like someone's fishing." Uncle Robb parks the truck near the boat launch, a small stretch of sand along the lake. They unload the kayaks, put on life vests, stow a paddle into each of the boats, and carry them down to the water. Taffy dashes down to the lake ahead of them. Robb holds her back from plowing in.

"Don't want a wet dog in my kayak, Taffy. You can swim when we come back."

Uncle Robb shows Maria where to place her hands on the paddle and she practices tipping it back and forth. He holds one of the boats, helps her to get into it, and tells her to rock back and forth gently to get the feel of it. Maria is quiet but smiles a little when the boat stays upright. Uncle Robb again demonstrates how to use the paddle and Maria practices until he is satisfied that she understands.

Uncle Robb pushes her boat just enough into the water so she is afloat. He holds his boat while Taffy jumps in and sits with her paws on the bow deck. Uncle Robb pushes his boat into the water and climbs in. He smiles at the comfortable feel of being in the boat again.

They paddle the two kayaks beside each other, close to the shore. The lake is surrounded by tall trees with a few houses tucked in among them. Pontoon boats are tied up at a couple of the docks.

"Am I doing this right? It keeps jerking from side to side." Maria frowns.

"Keep your body straight and move the paddles with your hands using the same pressure on each side."

Maria concentrates and then smiles. Her boat is now moving straight, not jerking from side to side.

Uncle Robb points toward the middle of the lake. Maria sees two black and white birds gliding around, with two smaller black and white birds bobbing beside them.

"Loons. They are here every year and have a nest over there." He points across the lake. "You can't see it unless you are very close. It is well-camouflaged."

They paddle past the fishing boat, keeping a polite distance. Uncle Robb waves to the two people fishing.

"Catch anything?"

"A few perch so far."

"Good luck."

Maria's arms are getting tired, but she is too excited to stop paddling. Uncle Robb lays his paddle across his kayak and lets his boat coast. Maria does the same. They drift for a few minutes.

Robb remembers that when he and Becca were first married, she had not been kayaking before. In the beginning she was uncertain about it, but she turned into an expert paddler and was willing to kayak anywhere.

Around a curve at the far end of the lake, Maria gasps. "Wow!" I have never seen such tall birds!" She points at two tall, gray birds with red patches on their heads who stand silently on the shore.

"Sandhill cranes." Uncle Robb stops paddling, steadying his boat away from shore.

After a few minutes he turns his boat and begins paddling back toward the other end of the lake. Maria pulls her phone out of her vest pocket and takes a picture of the tall birds to text to her mom and her sister. She wishes they were here.

They paddle slowly along the opposite side of the lake in a loop back to the boat launch.

"Watch the fallen logs along the shore that stick out into the lake. There are often turtles sitting along them." Uncle Robb points toward shore.

Maria looks carefully at every log they pass, but doesn't see any. She keeps looking as they slowly paddle by.

"Are those turtles over there?" Maria points.

"Sure enough. I think there are three of them."

At the other end of the lake, they drift a few minutes, enjoying the sparkle of the sun shining on the lake and the gentle breeze.

"Ready? You head in first all the way onto the beach, and I'll come in beside you."

Maria lands her kayak on the shore and raises her paddle in the air. "I did it!" She climbs out of the kayak and pulls it farther onto the beach. Uncle Robb's kayak drifts in beside hers. He gets out and pulls the kayak out of the water.

"Let's carry the boats up to the truck. I'll wipe them out while you throw the frisbee into the water for Taffy as she takes her swim."

Taffy follows them up to the truck and dances around when Maria grabs the frisbee. They run down to the water and Taffy plunges in. Maria throws the frisbee awkwardly at first. Taffy splashes through the water to retrieve it and bring it back.

Uncle Robb comes down and smiles as he watches their gleeful play.

They load the kayaks and stow the gear back in the truck. Maria gives Uncle Robb a shy hug.

"Thank you."

"My pleasure." He gently pats her back and then hands her a towel. She rubs Taffy all over to dry her off.

On the way home in the truck, Maria looks back at Taffy, who sits up proudly in the back seat.

"Do you think Taffy is lonely? That she misses her other family?"

"Maybe. But she has found another family with Tara, and with you. She seems happy enough."

"Good." Maria leans back in her seat and watches out the window. She looks thoughtful.

"You are worried about your mom and your sister?" Uncle Robb looks at her and then looks back at the road.

"Yes." A quiet voice.

"They are not safe in Mexico?"

"I don't know. We left our neighborhood because my parents could not find work, and there were drug gangs there. Now mi madre and mi hermana stay with one of my aunts and uncles. My dad lives somewhere else and sends them money when he finds work."

"Do you hear from them?"

"We text or call most days. They send pictures sometimes. My sister does not look very happy. She was so happy in school here. She was a really good student. I know she wishes she were here now. She had only two more years and then she wanted to go to college and become a marine biologist. It isn't fair. It should be her who is here and not me."

"Maybe it should be both of you."

Maria nods.

When Tara gets home, Maria tells her all about the kayak trip, how Taffy rode in Uncle Robb's boat, how they saw the tall, elegant cranes standing on the shore. After Maria goes to her room to text her mom and read before bed, Uncle Robb tells Tara how Maria is worried about the safety of her mom and sister. Tara wishes they could do something about that.

"At least we are keeping Maria safe," says Uncle Robb. He looks closely at Tara. "Everything okay? You have been pretty quiet since you got home from work. I guess I didn't notice at first because Maria was talking so excitedly about our kayak trip."

"It's not that serious really. Just something that happened at work."

"Which was…"

"I saw this kid, around ten years old, put a couple of small toys in his pocket. I watched to see if he was going to pay for them, but he just walked up to the front door. I wasn't sure if I should turn him in or just let him go. But I did not want him to think he could get away with it and then get into trouble doing it again later on."

"A dilemma. What did you decide?"

"I walked up quickly behind him and whispered that it would probably be a good idea to put the toys back."

"And did he?"

"He did. And he left the store quickly. I think he was embarrassed, and I felt badly about that. I wanted to buy him the toys, so he would not have to steal them."

"You did the right thing. He was only ten, and maybe was just trying out this behavior. But you kept him from getting in trouble, and hopefully he will think twice about doing it again."

"Thanks. I feel better."

Tara goes up to her room, gets ready for bed. She pulls the letters out of the journal and sorts them in order of earliest date first. She opens the first envelope and smooths out the letter.

Twenty-three

Letters from Miguel

7 August, 1971

Dear Rebecca,

I made it back to Nice. After my plane landed in Paris, I met this woman in the airport who was hitchhiking, and we decided to team up. Don't worry, I didn't sleep with her. But when I wasn't paying attention, she stole the money I had in my backpack. I guess I should have known better. Anyway, I had some money in my wallet that was in my pants pocket and a little bit of food left from our trip, but I had to ration it along the way.

It took me a couple of days to hitchhike back to Nice, but on the first day, I met a couple of French students who gave me a ride and let me sleep on their couch the first night. The next night I didn't really sleep, but I got a ride with a truck driver because he wanted someone to talk to him and help him stay awake. And he shared some of his lunch with me.

He was pretty interesting and had a lot of stories to tell about long-distance truck driving. He dropped me off close to Nice, and I had just enough money to take a train the last distance. It was good to get home, but I miss you. I can't wait until you come back to France and we will be together again.

This morning I got back to sorting the data for my dissertation. I think it's going okay. Wish you were here to distract me. Remember the list of the 100 ways to eat strawberries that you started? It is still on the blackboard in my room. I think about you and how you used to think up crazy recipes. You made me laugh and kept me sane when I was frustrated with sorting out the data and what it meant.

I think about the trips we took to Spain and all the sights we saw over the summer hitching around England, Scotland, and Wales. I'm sorry we argued sometimes. If we were together, I don't think we would do that.

Hope you made it home safely. I am watching for a letter. I miss you so much.

See you soon, I hope,

Love, Miguel

14 August 1971

Dear Rebecca,

I was happy to get your letter today! Glad you made it home safely, though you had some trouble flying standby from New York to home. How was your visit with Marianne? Did you stay at her house for a while? Did you do anything fun?

I guess your parents forgave you for hitchhiking around with some guy they don't know. At least they picked you up from the airport and bought you lunch. Ha, ha. Did you tell them about our summer travels? Did you say anything about wanting to go back to France? You could get a job here for a couple of years, maybe teach English.

What are you going to do for the rest of the summer? Will you laze around on the beach and get a good tan? Or can you go back to your old summer job for a few weeks? I hope you spend time thinking about me. I guess you still have to find a place to live for fall semester. Any leads on that?

Have you had a chance to contact your university to see if you can graduate a semester early so you can get back here to France to be with me? Or do you have to go down there in person?

Sorry to ask so many questions. I just miss you so much and hate not being able to see you every day and talk to you about everything.

Remember our friend from El Salvador? He decided to stay a few more weeks to work on his French. If he isn't taking other classes, he can take a French class and go out and talk to people. When you come back, you could do that for a few weeks, just to get more fluent in French.

We rode my Mobylette to the Italian border and back just for fun. He had never ridden one before.

Te amo, Miguel

21 August 1971

Dear Rebecca,

Getting a letter from you makes any day a wonderful day. I love hearing about what you are doing, although I don't want you to enjoy being home too much. Because I want you to miss being with me. I hope you miss me as much as I miss you.

I hear that a new crop of students on the same program you were on will be coming in September. I guess the profs enjoyed your group so much they have decided to do it again. Sounds like the group might be a bit bigger this time around. But in any case, you won't be in it! So sad for me. Anyway, they asked me to be a liaison person again. I did such a great job last time, don't you think? I could liaise with you anytime!

One of the professors who is overseeing my dissertation asked me to help out with some of his research. It pays a stipend, so I hope I can save some money for when you come back. We could maybe find a small apartment that we could afford, so it would just be the two of us. Imagine that we could be alone whenever we wanted. Not like when we lived in the Cité dorms.

We could both work, and I could finish my dissertation. Then we could go anywhere we wanted. Someday I want to move back to Latin America, but that wouldn't have to be right away. Where would you like to live? I wonder if you could use your teaching degree here in France or somewhere else. Would you have to go back to school, do you think?

You remember the guy from Thailand? I ran into him yesterday and he is planning to spend another semester here. I got my guitar and we went to a café and took turns playing songs. He is a really good player, so we drew a bit of a crowd. I am going to have to find some time to practice more. What about you? Have you been playing your guitar? Were you happy to get back to your real guitar?

Well, have to go and get supper at the Cité.

Don't forget me!

Te amo, Miguel

28 August 1971

Dearest Rebecca,

I have not gotten a letter from you this week. I hope that doesn't mean you are giving up on us, or that you have forgotten all about me. Are you getting ready to go back to school? Did you find a place to live? What classes are you taking?

I have been working a lot and sorting my data. I think I am about ready to analyze it and begin writing. I will be glad to get this over with. Wish you were here to give me a break from the grind.

I met a couple who bought a motorcycle and are riding around Europe. They graduated from college last May and worked for the summer. They were able to save up their money, so they could come to Europe, buy a motorbike, and travel around for a while. No itinerary, just going wherever they feel like going.

Maybe you and I should do that. There are lots of places I haven't seen yet, and I think you would enjoy places you didn't get to see when you were here. We could work for a while, save our money, and then take a trip like that before we moved wherever I got a teaching job. What do you think? Where would you like to go?

Also, our friend from Nigeria invited us to visit him whenever we want to. We could do some traveling in Africa before we settle somewhere.

Write to me!

Love, Miguel

4 September 1971

Dear Rebecca,

I got your letter, and something tells me you are not sure about coming back to France. You seemed more distant and didn't tell me much about what you are doing. Are you and Brian getting back together? I thought you told him it was over. Or have you met someone else?

As you can tell, I am worried that you are forgetting about me. But I have not forgotten you at all and am still waiting eagerly for you to come back and be with me. I will just assume that you were tired when you wrote or having trouble getting started back at school in the States.

Anyway, except for missing you, I am doing okay. My dissertation is coming along, and I plan to be done writing it before you get here so we have plenty of time together. My job is interesting, and my prof seems pleased with what I am accomplishing. He hinted that I might be able to get a job here. What would you think if we stayed in Nice for a while?

Last night I went with some of the French students to a movie. It was funny, and I think you would have liked it. Do you get French films at the U? We went out afterwards and stayed at the café until pretty late. Wish you had been with me.

Sorry this letter is short, but I have a meeting with my prof and have to get to work.

Don't forget me!

Te amo, Miguel

Tara refolds the last letter and slips it back into the envelope. She feels sad for Miguel. He seemed so excited about her aunt's return to France and their future together. But in his last letter it's clear he is worried that she has changed her mind. Making one last hopeful effort, he ends the letter as if all is well.

How did her aunt feel when she received this letter? Did she reply? It looks like Miguel did not write again. Tara wants to know more about what made her aunt decide not to return to be with Miguel.

What would she have done in that situation? Would she want to give up everything that was comfortable and go on an adventure, not knowing what it would be like? Or would she want to play it safe and stick with what she knew? Tara laughs at herself. So far, she has stuck with the safe options in her life.

Twenty-four

Summer 2023

"Guess we better water the seeds we planted. It hasn't rained, and our beans won't sprout if they dry out too much." Uncle Robb looks at the garden. Taffy watches from underneath a large shade tree, her head on her paws.

"I'll do it. Show me how," Maria says.

Uncle Robb unrolls the hose, turns on the water, and demonstrates the different choices with the spray nozzle. Then he hands the nozzle to Maria. Maria moves the sprayer slowly back and forth over the planted seeds.

"Hey." Jayden walks into the backyard. "Mr. Casey, I'm sorry but I can't mow the lawn today. My mom has to go to an appointment, and I have to take care of Hailey. How about tomorrow?"

"Tomorrow would be okay."

"We could probably take care of her." Maria looks at Uncle Robb.

"I guess we could. Bring your little sister over here for a while. I could probably even rustle up some toys."

"Really? You wouldn't mind? That would be a big help as I have a pretty full mowing schedule this summer, and I don't want to get behind. Baseball practice is at 4:00 today, and I can't miss that."

"Better keep to the schedule then. I look forward to your team winning a few games when I watch you guys this year."

"Thanks. We better win more than a few." Jayden laughs. "Anyway, can I bring Hailey over in an hour? I know she likes to come over here." Jayden stops. Hailey loved to come over especially to see Rebecca. He does not know what to say next, because his mom told him thinking about Rebecca makes Robb sad.

"I know." Robb nods to let Jayden know it's okay. "An hour will be fine. We'll have fun."

Jayden thanks them again, smiles shyly at Maria, and walks away.

"How old is Jayden's little sister?"

"Seven, I think."

"And you have toys somewhere?" Maria turns to Uncle Robb and accidentally sprays him with the hose. He jumps back just in time to keep from being soaked.

"Oh, I'm sorry. I got you wet."

"I'm fine. It's a warm day. Let's turn off the water, though. Looks like we have enough water on our garden." He looks down at the puddle of water at Maria's feet.

"Oops." Maria smiles when he says "our garden."

"We still have some of Tara's toys. Let's have some lunch and then go up in the attic and see what we can find that Hailey might play with."

"You have toys in the attic?"

"Tara stayed here a lot, and we always kept a lot of toys here for her. My wife…" Uncle Robb stops. For a moment he feels like she is just in the house, fixing lunch. He shakes his head. "Anyway, she could not bear to part with some of the books and toys. Those years when Tara was growing up were great fun for both of us." He sighs.

Maria follows him into the house and helps him to prepare sandwiches and lemonade. After lunch Uncle Robb leads her to the door at the end of the upstairs hallway. Taffy follows along behind them. Uncle Robb turns the wooden peg and opens the door.

The attic is dark and warm from the rays of the sun that peek through a dusty window. He pulls on a string that hangs from the ceiling. Dim light reveals neat rows of boxes and plastic cartons stacked along the walls. Floorboards creak as they walk across the floor.

"Here we are. I think everything is in these cartons." He gestures to the cartons under the window, lifts a lid and looks inside. "Yes, these are the ones. Let's carry them out into the hallway where we can see better." He picks up a carton, and Maria grabs a second one.

When Robb brings out the third carton, she is already looking at a carton of books. "Some of these books look kind of old. But there are lots of newer ones, too." Taffy sticks her nose into the box and sneezes.

"Come on, silly." Maria gently pulls Taffy back.

"Some of them Rebecca had when she was a kid. Tara loved to read those. Time travel, she used to say." He holds up Time Cat. "How about this one? Lloyd Alexander was a favorite, especially the Chronicles of Prydain series."

Maria picks up Time Cat and reads the first few pages. "I could read this to Hailey, if she likes books." She picks up another one. "How about Mouse on a Motorcycle?"

"Good idea. Let's see what's in these other cartons." He opens another one. "I remember when Tara used to love these."

Maria peers in and starts taking out little animals. "Calico Critters. Look, there are several animal families. Cute. And there is the house, too, and all kinds of furniture. I think Hailey will like these."

Maria opens the third carton. She finds crafty things like colored paper, pipe cleaners, tissue paper, stickers. "This looks fun, if Hailey likes crafty stuff."

They carry the boxes downstairs to the TV room. Maria looks with satisfaction at the toys she sets out for Hailey to choose from.

Maria sits on the front porch and waits for Jayden to bring Hailey over. He comes back in an hour with Hailey, who stands back a little.

"Hey. Thanks for helping us out." Jayden smiles.

"You're welcome." She smiles and looks at Hailey. "Hi, Hailey. I'm Maria. Uncle Robb and I found some toys and craft stuff we can do, if you want to."

"Okay."

"Hailey, I'm going to mow Mr. Robb's lawn, and when I'm done with the rest of my lawns, I'll be back to get you. Behave and do whatever Mr. Robb says."

Hailey rolls her eyes. "I always behave."

"We'll have fun."

"Great." Jayden nods to Maria. "See you later on then."

Maria and Hailey watch him mow the front yard for a few minutes, and then Maria takes Hailey into the living room to show her the toys. Hailey explores all the toys before choosing.

"We can do some paper flowers later, maybe?" Hailey looks up at Maria.

"Sure."

"Can we take the Calico Critters outside?"

"How about the back porch?"

Hailey nods. They set up the Calico Critters house, divide up the animal families, and begin to play a game that one of the baby animals Is having a birthday, and there will be a big party.

Jayden comes around to the back, mows the backyard, and tells Hailey he will be back soon. She waves but barely looks up as she continues playing with the Calico Critters.

Later in the afternoon, Tara hears voices from the backyard and goes around the house. She watches Maria rock the hammock back and forth while she reads to Hailey. Jayden sits cross-legged on the grass near the hammock, petting Taffy who lies beside him.

Tara recognizes the Lloyd Alexander book, Time Cat. A flash of memory reminds Tara of Aunt Rebecca.

Tara lay next to Aunt Rebecca in the hammock and looked up at the blue sky. She stroked the black kitten that slept curled up on her chest.

"Look, Aunt Rebecca, there's a dragon flying by." She pointed up and watched a large cloud drift across the sky. The sun winked out and then reappeared through the wispy clouds.

Aunt Rebecca looked up. "It does look like a dragon. And isn't that a unicorn?"

Tara laughed. "Maybe."

Aunt Rebecca began to read again. Tara watched clouds drift across the sky and listened. Her aunt finished the story and closed the book.

"Jason and Gareth were really lucky. They got to travel all over. Aunt Becca, do you think Jason ever saw any of those people again, like Gareth said he would?"

"Maybe. What do you think?"

"I think he did. Would you go to all those places that Jason and his cat went back then, if you could?"

"Maybe not all of them. How about you?"

"I would like to go to Egypt and see the pyramids and the sphinx. But I wouldn't want to meet a pharaoh or a king like Jason and Gareth did. The Egyptians did like cats, though, so they were not all bad. In Japan it was like that, too. They liked cats, but the Regent was not' very nice. The Emperor learned more about cats, though, and he turned out okay. I definitely wouldn't choose to go to Germany when they were killing witches and cats. That sounded pretty creepy. I would like to see the Incas in Peru. They had cool clothes, and I would like to see the llamas. What about you?"

"I agree with you. In general, I think I would like to travel in more modern times. Maybe to Europe, or Japan or Peru, or maybe Nepal or Bali. In all the stories, there seemed to be bad people who gave Jason and his cat a hard time, but also good people who were kind to them or helped them out."

"When I grow up, I'm going to travel around the world and see everything. It would be fun to travel with a cat like Gareth. Too bad Blackberry can't time travel like he did." Tara stroked the cat again. "But she was lucky, because we found her that night when it was raining and brought her inside and took good care of her."

"Blackberry is one lucky cat. I hope you get to travel as much as you want to. And enjoy your cat when you get home."

Those were good days, good memories. She and her aunt used to lie in the hammock every summer and read to each other. Books that are still memorable. Older books like Pippi Longstocking, The Boxcar Children, Nancy Drew, and The Hardy Boys from her aunt's collection. Then the Babysitter's Club and Harry Potter. Those times were magical, as she got lost in the stories. Sadness is mixed with gratitude for the time she spent exploring books with her aunt.

Tara sets her things down on the table by the door and goes into the kitchen. Uncle Robb is preparing his specialty, barbecued chicken for the grill.

"Looks delicious. You haven't made that for a while."

"It was time, I thought. One of your aunt's favorites."

Tara nods. "How did Jayden's sister end up here?"

"Jayden stopped by to say he would not be here to mow the lawn because his sister's childcare is closed for a week and his mom had to go to work. Maria said maybe we could take care of her, and I agreed we could do that. He has worked pretty hard since his dad died, to do his share. I try to do what I can for him."

"I'm glad you can help him out. And it looks like Maria enjoys taking care of Hailey."

"They both like to do crafts. We rummaged around in your aunt's things and found some crafty items." He points to some paper flowers in a vase on the table. "And in the process, we found a box of books. I remember you and your aunt reading together a lot in that hammock." He pauses, takes a deep breath. "I let them play with the Calico Critters. Hope that is okay."

"Sure." Tara puts an arm around him and gives him a hug. "Those were great times for me."

"I enjoyed every minute of it. Wish I could have it all back again. But time goes on."

"Looks like Jayden is interested in the story, too."

"When he came to pick up Hailey, Maria was reading to her and Hailey wanted to hear the rest of the story. So, Jayden said he would wait until they found a breaking point.

In a few minutes, Maria calls through the screen door that she is going to walk Hailey and Jayden back to their house. When dinner is ready, Tara goes to the front door to see if Hailey is on her way home. When she hears voices, she stops. Maria and Jayden sit on the porch steps.

"And my mom and my sister were deported, just like that." Maria snaps her fingers.

"That's terrible." Jayden looks at Maria with concern. "You miss them, I bet."

Maria nods. "Tara told me about your dad. I'm really sorry."

"Thanks. It's been hard, and I still think about him a lot. But my mom and my sisters and me are really close and we take good care of each other."

Tara quietly closes the door. Maria and Jayden sound so open about their grief, able to move on at the same time. Maybe she and her uncle are doing that, too.

Twenty-five

Tara rings up sales at the register. When Anna comes in and takes over, Tara restocks some toys that have been selling fast. As she lines up some toy boats on the shelf, she hears a sniffling sound in the back of the store and then a choked-back sob. She leans back and scans the area where it came from. A boy who looks to be about four years old stands by himself, rubbing his eyes. Tara doesn't see an adult nearby, so she walks over to him.

"Hello, are you okay? Where is your mom or dad? Or your grandma?"

The boy shakes his head. "I can't find her."

Tara kneels down to eye level. "Did she come in the store with you?"

He shrugs. "I thought she was right behind me. But I don't see her anywhere."

"She was with you before you came into the toy store?"

"She was pushing the stroller with my little sister in it."

"Well, let's walk around the store and see if we can find her." She holds out her hand and he puts his hand in hers.

"My name is Tara."

"I'm Lucas."

To distract him, Tara points out toys that might interest Lucas as they walk slowly around the store. He is interested in the Lego sets, especially the one with a picture of a dragon on the box. The store is not very big, and soon they stand by the front door. Through the window, Tara sees a woman with a stroller, looking frantically up and down the sidewalk. Lucas watches her.

"Could that be your mom?"

Lucas nods and beams a big smile. Tara opens the door and walks outside with him.

"You found him! Thank you. I was so worried." The woman looks like she is not sure whether to hug Lucas or yell at him. She hugs him. "You scared me. You need to make sure you stay by me." She turns to Tara. "Thank you again."

Tara goes back into the store and finishes stocking the toy boats.

When she gets home, she finds her uncle in the kitchen, unloading a bag of groceries. She picks up a box of chili pepper lights. "Where did these come from?"

"The garden store. Maria wanted to plant flowers along the walkway before the party. We went there to pick up a flat. When we walked down the aisle to the flower section, she pointed out those lights and said they reminded her of the lights her mom always put up in the yard for birthday parties. So, I bought some, of course." He smiles, and Tara realizes that she has seen him smile much more often lately.

"Good idea. I have been thinking about decorations for the party. Lights will be perfect."

Uncle Robb frowns. "Maria was excited about the lights, but after I left her to pick out the flowers while I grabbed a bag or two of mulch, she seemed upset. I thought she might be sad about her mom not being here for her birthday, so I didn't press her. And then she told me about an incident at the garden store. When we got home, she went straight to her room, and I haven't heard anything from her since. Maybe you should go see if she is okay."

"What incident?"

"Maybe you should ask her."

Tara frowns. "Okay. I'll go see if I can help. Thanks for getting the lights and the flowers."

Tara goes upstairs and listens at the door of Maria's room. It is silent. She knocks gently.

"Maria, may I come in?" She waits for a response.

Then a quiet, "Okay."

Tara opens the door. Maria sits on her bed and watches the birds fly from tree to tree outside the window. Tara sits down beside her.

"The lights and flowers you picked out will be great for the party."

Maria nods.

"Everything okay?"

Maria shakes her head.

"Did something happen?"

Maria nods again.

"Tell me about it?"

Maria takes a deep breath. "When I was picking out the flowers, there were two women watering plants, talking in Spanish. I was happy to hear them because it reminded me of my mom. So, I said something to them in Spanish. They smiled at me and we began talking."

"That sounds good."

"But then these two older men walked by and said something like, 'Wetbacks. Why don't you stay in your own country?' They looked angry."

"Then what happened?"

"The three of us looked at each other, but we didn't say anything to those men. The women ignored those men and went back to work, and I hurried to find Uncle Robb."

"That's terrible. Those men had no right to do that."

"What's a wetback?"

"It's a stupid term. I haven't heard people say it much anymore. People say it to describe Mexicans who wade across the Rio Grande, often at night, to get to the U.S. and try to avoid the border guards."

"Oh. That is stupid." Maria shakes her head. "That is not how my family came here. We didn't get wet at all."

"Of course not."

"Uncle Robb got pretty mad about it when I told him. I thought he was going to go find those guys and tell them off. I've never seen him mad like that, and I liked him for wanting to stand up for me. He thought maybe it wasn't a good idea, though. There being two of them and much younger than him."

"He and my aunt are/were always willing to speak up against prejudice. I'm sorry you have to put up with stuff like that."

"Uncle Robb says we have to rise above it and go on our way. Do the right thing even if they don't."

"Good advice." Tara stands up. "Want to help make tacos for dinner?"

"Okay." Maria follows Tara downstairs.

Uncle Robb adds onions and peppers to a can of black beans and heats up tortillas, no need for meat in tacos. Tara shreds cheese and cuts up fresh fruit. Maria says she will make the salsa and the guacamole, her family's special recipes. The aroma of the green, earthy smell of the avocado and the tang of the cilantro scents the room.

During dinner Maria is quiet again. She looks down at her plate and picks at her food.

Tara wonders what she can say that might help Maria forget about the mean guys at the garden store. What would it be like to be minding your own business and have people say mean things to you just because you aren't just like them? A memory flashes into her mind. When she was ten, she was building a sand castle on the beach, and a boy came up to her and said she was fat. Her aunt looked him right in the eye and said, "That was unkind." The boy ran off down the beach, and Tara felt safe, protected.

"Did you tell Tara about the trauma dog at the garden store?" Uncle Robb looks at Maria.

Maria looks up. "You mean the dog who is suffering from the war in Afghanistan?"

"Yes. He sometimes comes to work with the person who adopted him, because she is helping him to be more relaxed around people."

"I almost forgot about him. Bailey." Maria's face lights up. "I saw him and I was going to pet him, but he put his head down and moved away from me. The woman working with the flowers told me all about him. She said I should be patient with him. I knelt down and reached out my hand just a little. And he finally came over and sniffed it. Then he let me touch his head just for a second. After that he followed me around the garden center. And I talked to him and told him all about my mom and my sister."

"Sounds like you made a friend. That was kind of you."

"Maybe we should invite him over to play with Taffy." Maria grins.

"Maybe we should." Tara smiles back.

Twenty-six

Maria and Jayden lean against the side of the brick building, which is closed and dark. The sun has just set, and dusk creeps in as the golden light fades. One streetlight is on farther down the road, but in this commercial area most of the buildings are unlit. To avoid being seen, they stand away from the small overhead light outside the front door that pierces the darkness. A car's headlights flash as it speeds past. Otherwise, all is quiet, except for a faint hum coming from an air conditioner. A soft breeze, cooling the heat from the afternoon sun, wafts over them. Maria shivers.

"You cold?" Jayden looks over at her.

"No, just nervous. Do you think they'll come? My friend Carlos said it was usually around this time of day, but something might have happened along the way."

"Something could have slowed them down. Have to wait and see."

Maria nudges Jayden and nods toward the black van driving down the street toward them. All the windows are blacked out except the front windshield. She can see a driver, but no passenger beside him in the front seat.

"Is that them?" Jayden nods toward the van.

"Looks like it. Carlos said it would be black." Maria whispers, even though there is no one nearby.

They stand up and watch the van turn into the driveway. It pulls up to the side of the building, and the driver jumps out of the front seat, leaving the door open. He unlocks the back door of the van, gestures for people to get out quickly, quickly, speaking in Spanish. People slowly climb out of the back of the van, looking exhausted and confused. When everyone is out, the driver hops into the van and tears out of the parking lot.

"How did they cram all those people in there? Why did he just leave them here?"

"With great difficulty. Poor people."

Maria and Jayden walk slowly toward the people who stand where the van used to be, clustered together, uncertain what to do.

"Agua! Bocados!" Maria calls out, holding up bottles of water in each hand. In Spanish she explains that she and Jayden have come to help with water and snacks. At first people look at them cautiously. But the need for food and water wins them over, and some of them shuffle toward Maria, legs stiff from the cramped space.

Suddenly, three cars and a windowless van careen into the parking lot and screech to a halt. Doors open and ICE agents pile out, shouting at the people from the van to get down on the ground.

Maria yells in Spanish, and one of the ICE men grabs her and pushes her toward the wagon. Jayden runs up and grabs his arm.

"Stop! You're making a mistake. Maria isn't illegal. She's a citizen!"

The ICE agent halts and glares at Jayden. "Take your hand off my arm and get out of here before I arrest you."

Jayden quickly pulls back his arm. "But you can't take Maria."

The man looks at Maria. "Birth record? Passport? Proof of citizenship?"

Maria shakes her head, eyes wide.

The agent walks away, pulling Maria with him. Maria looks back at Jayden, tears in her eyes. Will she be deported? Where will they send her? How will she find her mom and her sister?

"No," Jayden shouts. "She was born here." Jayden runs his fingers through his hair.

The ICE man pushes Maria into the group of people they hustle into the van.

"Maria, I'm going to call your uncle. We'll get you out of there." Jayden dashes to the other side of the building, out of the way of the cops. He pulls out his cell phone and taps on Robb's phone number. Thank goodness he put Robb's number in his phone in case he needed to call about lawn mowing. The phone rings. "Come on, answer, hurry." Jayden paces back and forth.

"Jayden? What can I do for you? Is everything all right?"

"They've taken Maria. You've got to come."

"What? Taken her where? Who's taken her?"

"The ICE cops. They think she's illegal. I tried to tell them she isn't, but they wouldn't listen. I think they're taking her to the jail."

"I'm not following this, but you can explain later. I'm going to call a friend who is a lawyer. Where are you?"

Jayden explains.

"I'll pick you up. Don't move. Stay right there."

"Uncle Robb, what's happened? Is Maria with Jayden?" Tara stands in the doorway.

"Some mix-up about Maria being illegal. I'm calling John. He's a lawyer and he'll know what to do." Robb is on the phone for a few minutes, explaining what little he knows about the situation. John agrees to meet them at the jail and suggests that Robb find Maria's birth certificate.

"I'll pick up Jayden and we'll meet John at the jail to spring Maria. Do you think you could find Maria's birth certificate? Where would she keep it?" Robb grabs his car keys from the hall table.

"I'll look through her things here, and if I don't find the document, I'll find the keys to grandma's house and look there. What's going on? Why would they think Maria is illegal?" Tara wanted to scream. How could the cops do this to someone like Maria?

"I won't know until I get to the jail. John will help sort it out. See you there in a few." Robb charges out the door and she hears his car peel out of the driveway.

Tara runs upstairs and looks around Maria's room. Where might she keep a birth certificate? Maria's purse is lying on the dresser. Might she keep it with her, ever fearful of ICE? Hating to invade Maria's privacy, Tara dumps out the items in the purse. No birth certificate. She unzips the compartment along the back of the purse. Just a comb and a coupon for an ice cream cone. Not here. She picks up the keys to grandma's house and puts them in her pocket.

On her way to grandma's house, Tara taps her fingers on the steering wheel. What if she can't find it? Would ICE really keep Maria? Impossible.

Tara parks the car in the driveway and dashes to the front door. In an alcove off the kitchen, she opens the two drawers in a small desk. A few folders of paid bills, an address book, a few business cards clipped together. No documents.

In the living room Tara opens the small drawer in an end table. Nothing of note. Upstairs she looks in Maria's small bedroom. No birth certificate in the dresser or in the closet. She opens a couple of shoe boxes on the closet floor. Only shoes.

Grandma's room is tidy, everything put away where it belongs. On the top shelf of the closet are a couple of sweaters and an extra blanket. Back in the corner she spies an old-fashioned flowered hat box. She can't resist a look at what kind of hat grandma would keep in there. When she pulls it down and opens it up, she finds all the legal documents, including Maria's birth certificate.

Tara tucks the birth certificate in her purse and rushes back to her car. When she pulls up at the jail, she sees her uncle's car already there. Jayden paces back and forth in the lobby, and he grabs her arm in relief.

"Robb and John somebody got through to the back when John told the man at the desk that he is Maria's lawyer. But they won't let me see her."

Tara goes up to the reception window. "I have a birth certificate that I need to give to someone. John Worth, Maria's lawyer, is back there and needs it for proof of citizenship."

"I'll call back and tell them it's here." The man at the desk picks up the phone and calls. In a few minutes, an ICE agent comes out front and takes the birth certificate.

"Don't lose it." Tara hands it to him.

"I know what I'm doing." He takes the birth certificate, turns and walks back the way he came.

Tara looks at Jayden. "Don't worry. John and my uncle will sort it out. Tell me what happened. Why did they pick up Maria?"

"Maria heard from her friend Carlos that a black van was headed toward Traverse City and would be carrying undocumented immigrants. I don't know how he got this information, but it sounded believable. He said this had happened before and told us where the van would most likely stop. Maria was worried about these people and wanted to do something to help them. I couldn't let her go alone, so we bought some water and snacks and decided to meet the van and help the people find somewhere to stay."

When he is done talking, he stops and takes a deep breath. He looks at Tara. "I know, I know. Now it sounds ludicrous, but it made sense at the time."

Tara nods and pats his arm. She can imagine how the idea of helping undocumented immigrants had appealed to Maria. Jayden was a kind kid and would want to help.

They sit on a bench by the window, both looking at their phones to pass the time. After about an hour, they look up and see John and Robb coming with Maria. Robb's arm is around her and he is murmuring something to her. Her eyes are red from crying, but she looks angry, Tara notes with surprise. She has not seen Maria angry before. Tara stands and Maria collapses into her arms.

"I'm sorry. I didn't mean to cause all this trouble. I just wanted to help those people. They are just looking for a better chance in life. Now after all they've been through, they will probably be sent back."

"You wanted to do something to help. A good intention." Tara looks at John, her eyebrows raised. Is all well? He nods.

When they get home, Maria says goodnight and goes up to her room. John stays for a few minutes while the three of them discuss what happened.

"Maria is safe, she is a U.S. citizen, but she needs to be careful about getting in the middle of these things. ICE might be harsher if it happens again." John shakes his head.

"We'll talk to her in the morning. She meant well." Robb walks John to the door. "Thanks again."

"Are you worried about what Maria might do? Do you want me to find another place for her to stay?"

"Not at all. I like having her here, and it makes me feel useful to have someone who needs me."

Tara smiles at him. "Thanks. You know I'll always need you, too." She goes upstairs to make sure Maria is all right. When she opens the door, she sees that Maria is already asleep.

Twenty-seven

Uncle Robb reads in the living room as Tara lets Taffy into the kitchen from the yard. The doorbell rings. Taffy follows Tara to the front door. On the porch stands a young man she doesn't know. He is good-looking, with curly dark brown hair, brown eyes. Tall, fit.

"Are you selling something?"

"Uh, no." He looks surprised and then laughs. "Of course, you don't know me. My name is Brent, Brent Delgado. I feel a bit foolish, but I had to come."

Tara frowns, unsure where this is leading.

"Sorry. If I could come in for a few minutes, I could explain. Here. This might give you some indication of why I'm here." He holds up an envelope. She opens the door and takes it. It is addressed to her aunt at this address. The return address is from someone named Miguel. The Miguel, Tara wonders. How could that be?

"As you can see, the letter is for Rebecca. Does she still live here?"

Tara shakes her head. "I guess you should come in. Rebecca is, was, my aunt. She died a couple of months ago."

"Oh, I'm so sorry. I was really hoping to meet her. I thought what the letter says would be important to her. This is really awkward."

She holds the door open for him. "Come in. I'm not sure what my uncle will think about it, but I guess he should hear what you have to say."

He follows her into the living room, but Tara stops him before he enters the room. "One second. I need to explain."

Standing in the doorway to the living room, she looks at her uncle. He is looking out the window at the flower garden, her aunt's garden.

"Uncle Robb, there is a man named Brent here to see us. He has a letter addressed to Aunt Rebecca. I asked him to come in. Is that okay?"

Her uncle looks at her in surprise. "I don't understand."

"I'm not sure that I do either. But he says he will explain. Is that okay?"

Her uncle nods. Tara gestures Brent into the room and introduces him.

Brent walks over and shakes hands. "Thank you for seeing me. It looks as if I have come at an awkward time. I am sorry for your loss. My uncle died a few weeks ago, and I know what a great loss a person can be."

"I'm sorry about your uncle. Please sit down." Uncle Robb gestures to the sofa. "How do you happen to have a letter addressed to my Rebecca?"

Brent takes a deep breath. This has turned out to be more complicated than he thought it would be. "After my uncle died, I offered to go through his things and decide what to do with them. My mom is very sad that her brother is gone, and I wanted to make things easier for her. Also, I am the executor of his estate. My uncle never married or had children of his own. He and I were very close. When I was going through his papers and things, I found this letter. He wrote it a few years ago, but clearly never sent it. I am not sure why. I wasn't sure if I should read it, as I did not want to invade his privacy. But

I thought maybe it was important, and I should honor whatever mattered to him."

"I noticed that the name on the return address is Miguel. Is that The Miguel that my aunt writes about in her journals from France?" Tara looks at him.

Brent smiles and lets out his breath, relieved that this woman seems to know something about what he is going to share with them. "Yes, I think it is. I know that my uncle studied in France in the 1970s and got his master's degree there. He never talked about it much, but he remained fluent in French while he was alive."

"My aunt writes as if she and this Miguel were an item in France, as if they were in love with each other. But she came back to the States, and they exchanged a few letters. Obviously, she eventually married my uncle." She smiles at Uncle Robb. "And they were very much in love."

"I don't know much beyond what my uncle says in this letter. I will leave it with you if you like, and you can see for yourself. I once asked him why he never married, had he ever been in love. He told me he had met the love of his life in France when he was young, but the timing was wrong and it didn't work out. That's why I thought maybe this letter was important."

"What happened to your uncle? Did he come back from France?"

"He came back to the States, got a law degree, passed the bar, and worked for a law firm in New York City for a while. When he thought he had enough experience, he headed for Latin America. He spent several years there, defending people who were political prisoners, Indigenous people, or were being treated unjustly. When his parents in Chicago got older and needed some help, he came back to the States and practiced law there while helping his parents out. It looks like that's when he wrote this letter."

Tara looks over at her uncle. She can see he is tired and has tears in his eyes. She stands up.

"It was kind of you to come all this way. Perhaps we could talk more tomorrow? Give me a phone number where you can be reached, and I will call you."

"Yes, of course." Brent looks startled but stands up quickly. "I'm sorry. I guess I wasn't thinking. This could be a bit of a shock. Thank you both for listening to me." He follows Tara to the door and enters his contact information when she hands him her phone.

"I hope that wasn't too much for your uncle." He looks at Tara with concern.

"He'll be okay. He knew about Miguel, or at least that there had been someone in France. He and my aunt were very happy together. But he sometimes still feels lost without her."

Brent nods. "I hope we get to talk more, but I understand if you decide not to."

Tara smile. "I am interested in talking more with you about my aunt and your uncle, and I will call you."

"Great. I look forward to it."

Tara waves to Brent as he gets into his car and backs it down the driveway. In the house she walks over to her uncle who sits in his chair, looking down at his hands. He looks up at her.

"I just miss her so much. When I met her, I knew there was someone she had not gotten over. But I gave her time, and I know she came to love me."

"I know she did, more than anyone." Tara hugs him, still holding the letter. "What should I do with this? Do you want to read it?"

Uncle Robb shakes his head. "You read it, if you want to." He stands and walks out into the flower garden.

Tara puts the letter upstairs on the nightstand. She is worried about Uncle Robb, wishing the letter had not been delivered. But she admires Brent for taking the time to do what he thought his uncle wanted after his death. She will probably read the letter, but right now she needs to try to make things more normal for her uncle. She goes downstairs to start dinner.

In a few minutes Uncle Robb joins her in the kitchen. She looks at him with concern, but can tell he is not ready to talk about this. She talks to him about work, telling him a funny story about one of the customers.

"Maria's birthday is just a few days away. What could we do to make it fun?"

"I don't know. Did you ask her what she wants to do?"

"I tried, but she just shrugged and said it didn't really matter."

"Ah. But, of course, it does matter. We'll think of something."

"Maria has outgrown some of her summer clothes. I could take her shopping to pick out a couple of new things."

"She'd like that, I think. I already bought gardening gloves for her, her own garden trowel, and a hat to wear to keep off the sun. I put them in a gift bag and hid it in my closet." He looks at her and shrugs his shoulder.

Tara laughs. "Looks like you're ahead of me."

"On her birthday we could visit her grandma, take a flowering plant and a cake."

"Good idea."

"Maybe we could ask Jayden to come over for pizza and cake."

"Let's invite the whole family. They've been my neighbors for years. Hailey adores Maria, and Maria could get to know the older sister. Could help when she starts school here in the fall."

"The four kids could find something fun to do. Maybe Jayden could invite a couple of his friends."

Maria and Taffy rush into the kitchen in a gush of energy and fresh air.

"You should have seen Taffy at the park. Jayden threw a stick really high by mistake, and Taffy jumped right up in the air to catch it. We were both surprised. Taffy must have liked it because she brought the stick right back to him, dancing around him. So, then he did it again. Jayden says Taffy is really an athlete." Maria laughs and catches her breath. "Jayden taught me how to throw the stick like that, and Taffy caught it over and over." Maria pats the dog on her head.

Uncle Robb and Tara both smile. Tara bends down and puts her arms around Taffy. "What a great dog you are."

After dinner Maria goes out on the back porch to text her sister. Uncle Robb and Tara go for a walk through the neighborhood. People wave or say hi and ask Uncle Robb how he is doing. He says he's coping, but doesn't stop to chat.

Back at home, Uncle Robb goes into the living room and picks up the book he has been reading. At least Tara thinks he is reading.

She looks at the number Brent typed into her phone. Should she call him? Did she want to talk more about this Miguel or just let things be? She is intrigued by the story of Miguel and Rebecca and is interested to hear more about Brent. She hesitates a few seconds and then selects his phone number. He answers right away, as if he was waiting for her call.

"Hi, this is Tara."

"Oh, hi. Thanks for calling. I felt like an idiot after I left your house. I hope I didn't upset your uncle."

"He seems okay. Grieving for my aunt is a long process. Some days are better than others. But I have been reading my aunt's journal from when she was a student in France. I would like to meet with you to talk more about that."

"Great. I would like that, too. It was a big surprise to me when my uncle told me about your aunt not long before he died. Where should we meet?"

"Do you know where the open area is along the bay? There is a big flower bed there and volleyball sand lots. We could walk a bit, maybe go for coffee."

"Sounds good. What time? I am here for a few days seeing a friend."

"How about tomorrow around 4:00? I get off work then and could meet you."

"Sure. I will see you there. By the garden?"

"Yes."

After dinner Tara sits on her bed, holding the letter that Miguel wrote to her aunt. Should she read it? She has read the journal, so reading the letter wouldn't be that much different. But she feels anxious about what it might say. Slowly, she opens the envelope, pulls out the letter, and smooths it.

Dear Rebecca,

Please read this letter even though you haven't heard from me for a long time. I regret that I stopped writing to you so long ago, and I want to explain.

When I went to France, I intended to get my Master's degree and perfect my French. I meant to return to the States and get a law degree, then go back to Latin America and help those who did not get fair treatment.

Then I met the love of my life. That being you, Rebecca. I was devastated when you got on that plane to return home because I was afraid that I would never see you again. I kept writing to you, hoping that, somehow, we could find a way to be together, and for a while that still felt possible.

When I stopped hearing from you, I considered writing and trying to persuade you that we could make a life together, but I realized that we would probably make each other miserable, wanting different things. From what you said in your last letter to me, I could tell that you had doubts about us. That made me sad, but I realized that you were not ready for a life with me.

Through the internet I found information about you, your marriage and career. I found this address. I hope this is still where you live.

I never married and had a family. I kind of regret that, but no woman ever compared to you, and I was always focused on the work I was doing, thinking I was making a difference in the world. I feel satisfied with how I have lived my life, but I want you to know how much you always meant to me.

I hope you are well and are satisfied with the choices that you made in life.

All my love and best wishes,
Miguel

Tara reads the letter once and then reads it through again. What would her aunt have thought if she had received this letter? Did she regret not sticking with Miguel? Did she ever wish she had chosen a life with him? If she had moved to Latin America, Aunt Becca and Uncle Robb would never have been such an important part of Tara's life.

If her aunt had read this letter, would she have left her uncle for him? No, Tara doesn't think so. Her aunt clearly loved her uncle dearly. She would never have hurt him like that. She wonders if her uncle would want to read the letter, but decides she will put it away and let him ask her if he wants to know about it.

Twenty-eight

Tara walks to the open space and scans the garden. Brent is already there, leaning against the raised bed of yellow, orange and white flowers that spell out TC 23. He looks up and waves to her. He smiles as he watches her walk across the park. The sun tries to peek through the white haze that covers the sky. Sometimes it succeeds, and shadows dance through the leaves of the trees.

"How was work?"

"Okay. It's getting busier all the time, but I'm starting to know my way around."

"I never asked. Where do you work?"

"At the toy store downtown."

"That sounds fun. Do you get to play much?"

"Not as much as I would like." She laughs. "What did you do today?"

"My friend Eric took me to see all the sights, like a regular tourist. Beaches, there are a lot of those, a couple of wineries and a brewery, a lot of those also. Of course, Sleeping Bear Dunes."

"Did you climb the big dune?"

"We did. Eric said it is a rite of passage, whatever that means, so we had to do it. Then we walked across to the bluff to look at the big lake. The sand was a bit hot, but the view at the end was worth the effort. Do you want to walk or sit somewhere?"

"Let's walk down to the marina and along the bay. Another area you have to see to be a real tourist."

Brent laughs. "After today, I can probably claim to be one."

"Tell me more about your uncle and his letter." Large sailboats rock gently in their slips as they walk past the marina.

"When my uncle found out he had cancer and it was incurable, he decided not to undergo treatment because, although it would prolong his life a little, he didn't want to end his life feeling miserable from the treatment. He decided to enjoy what time he had left as much as he could and set about making up for anything he thought he had not done right in the past."

"That's interesting. My aunt was one of the things he thought he had not done right?"

"I'm not sure. He started contacting people he thought he had not been fair to or had not kept in touch with. He had always been busy and sometimes didn't stay in touch. Near the end of his life, he wanted family and friends to know how much they mattered to him."

"Sounds like a good way to spend his time at the end of his life. Sad, though."

"Agreed. His time in France seemed to be on his mind. He started telling me about the people he met while he was there, the traveling he did. And what an idealist he had been when he was young. Your aunt seemed to play a very large role in his time in France."

"I have been reading the journals my aunt wrote when she was in France, and I learned a lot about her life while she was there. Your uncle was very important to her. They were both so young, really. And it was such a different time in the world."

"Different but still a lot the same?"

"Yes, I'd say that. Did your uncle say why he and my aunt didn't get together again? After she left to come home to the States. My aunt seemed undecided about it, but then the relationship seemed to end."

"My uncle said, as I mentioned, that he was an idealist. He thought he could change the world. Make it better. To him that meant standing up for people who were oppressed or were being treated unfairly. He wanted to dedicate himself to that and did not think it would work for your aunt. Not that he thought she didn't care about such things. But he knew how much she missed home, her family and friends. He didn't want to take her away from all that."

"She made a life for herself, helping to make life better for other people. She certainly saved me many times. And family was always very important to her. I know she and my uncle really loved each other, and they made each other happy."

"Can't do better than that." Bent smiles at her. "What did your uncle think about the letter? Perhaps I should have mailed it. But I wasn't sure that the address was correct. And I was coming up here anyway. I shouldn't have sprung it on him like that. Honestly, I didn't mean to do that."

"He seems okay with it. He gave me the letter to do whatever I wanted to with it. He has been grieving a lot, but I think one conclusion he came to was that my aunt was sincere in that she loved him, chose him."

"Great. I'm sure he deserves that. So, did you?"

"Did I what?"

"Read the letter."

"Course." She laughs. "Just nosy, I guess. Couldn't let the opportunity go by to find out more. My aunt and your uncle had one of those appealing love stories."

"I thought so, too."

In the water park, kids shriek as they dash through the fountain spouting up in the air. On the beach people wade in the still-cold water or lie on blankets in the sun.

"Some pretty big boats tied up in the marina. What's that big boat way over there?"

"Coast Guard. They have a training school here."

"There are lots of tourists here in the summer?"

Tara frowns. "Too many sometimes, but it's a beautiful area."

"Do you like living in a tourist town?"

"I spent a lot of time here when I was growing up. It seemed exciting to me then. I like lots of things about it, but not sure about all the touristy stuff."

"Where would you like to live, if you could live anywhere in the world?"

Tara laughs. "That's a tough question. Let me think. Of course, there are lots of places I haven't been. But two places I loved when I visited them were Hawaii and Costa Rica. What about you? Do you already have a place picked out?"

"Sort of. Costa Rica is definitely a favorite. I could like Hawaii a lot, I think."

"What about your job? Would you move somewhere and start over?"

"Haven't figured all that out yet. A lot of what I do can be done on the computer, but the best part of the job is actually meeting with people. Just dreaming maybe of living in a beautiful place."

"Sounds like me. I'm ready to start something new, sort of forced into thinking about it during the pandemic. But I'm not sure what or where."

"Good to keep the options open, I think."

"Agreed. We should probably head back." Tara turns around, and they walk back along the beach to the marina and back to the garden where they started.

Brent looks at her. "It was great to talk with you and find out more about your aunt. Maybe we could do it again before I leave in a few days."

"Sure." Tara smiles.

Brent gives her a long look. He holds out his hand, and when she takes it, he holds it a bit longer than necessary.

Tara turns and walks away. She gives in to the temptation to look back, and when she does, Brent is watching her. She waves and he waves back.

Twenty-nine

Two days later, Tara has not heard from Brent. Should she call him? She remembers her aunt's journal entry about the etiquette of a girl calling a boy. Maybe he's not sure either about contacting her again. She finds his number on her phone.

"Hello."

"Hi, this is Tara." She hesitates.

"Great, glad you called. I thought about calling, but thought maybe I should give you some space. Didn't want to be too pushy."

"How about a hike up Alligator Hill? Is that too pushy?"

Brent laughs. "Just right. Didn't know you had alligators around here. Thought they liked the warmer climes." She hears a smile in his voice. "Wouldn't mind seeing one or two, though, from a distance."

Tara laughs. "Very funny. It's just that the hill looks like an alligator, I guess. There is a great view from the top."

"I'm in."

"How about today? I have the day off."

"Great. What time?"

"How about 11:00? We'll eat sandwiches for lunch at the top."

"Should I bring something?"

"No, not this time." Then she worries that she is implying there will be more times.

"Next time, then."

Tara likes the sound of that. "I'll pick you up by the garden, if that's okay."

"I'll be there."

When she pulls up in the car by the garden at 11:00, Brent is waiting on the sidewalk. She is glad to see he is wearing appropriate hiking shoes.

On the drive to the hike, Brent asks questions about the places they pass.

"Looks like this is farming country, lots of corn fields."

"You know something about farming?"

"Just used to traveling a lot and noticing things. Interested in how we get our food, I guess."

Tara nods. She points out the small town they are passing through. "This is Cedar. That little farm stand there is a great place for strawberries and peaches."

"No one seems to be there to take your money."

"That's one of the things I like. You just take what you want and put your money in that red box with the slot in it."

"Unique."

Not far from Cedar, they pass through Maple City, and Brent comments on the number of new houses being built.

As the car turns a corner, Brent suddenly yells, "Watch out!"

Tara steps hard on the brakes. "What is it?" And then she sees the small fawn standing in the middle of the road. "Oh! It's so small I didn't even see it."

The fawn darts across the road and into the trees.

"I hope its mom is nearby."

"Hope so. Looks too young to be on its own."

At the trail parking lot, Tara pulls out her pack out of the car. Brent reaches for it and she lets him take it. She knows she is perfectly capable of carrying it herself, but it feels good to have him offer.

"Hey, what are those?" He points to several cement shed-like structures on the left of the path.

"Something to do with charcoal, I think."

"Here it is on the Sleeping Bear sign." Brent reads aloud. "These concrete structures, located at the trailhead on Stocking Drive, are kilns built in the 1950s by lumberman Pierce Stocking. The sawmill he set up near this spot produced considerable waste that was converted into charcoal in these kilns. The loose, dusty, random-sized material was packed in bags for shipment to stores in much of Michigan for sale to campers and picnickers.

The kilns are concrete ovens in which limbs, slabs, and other sawmill waste were stacked as tightly as possible. The open front was closed with concrete blocks and the wood set on fire just before the last blocks went in. Controlling the air intake was tricky: too much air and the wood was consumed, too little air and the fire went out. If successful, the fire burned slowly for several days. Once it was out, the charcoal was removed and spread to cool. Then it was moved to the bagging shack."

"That explains it thoroughly." Tara laughs. "When Aunt Becca brought me here, I thought it was weird to see charcoal furnaces in the midst of this beautiful area."

"I wonder what the area was like back then."

The path rises slightly up to the main trail where a sign by the path has an arrow that points in both directions and says "loop."

"Which way?"

"Left. I like coming back on the right side of the loop because I can come straight down the trail. When I was a kid, I used to run part of the way."

They climb the upward sloping trail. At a spot where a little used trail veers off to the right, Tara stops and points to the glint of water through the trees.

"There's Lake Michigan. In the summer you can see only a glimmer of it on this part of the trail. But in the winter the water blinks through the bare trees more often."

"Nice. We'll have to come back in the winter."

Tara smiles. "The view is even better at the top."

"Let's go, then." He starts running up the hill and she runs to catch up with him. After a short run, they both stop, taking deep breaths. "Maybe save the running for downhill."

They continue walking, not talking for a while. On the right they pass a bench where a couple sits close together, holding hands.

Brent smiles at Tara. "So, you came here with your aunt? She liked to hike, I guess."

"She hiked as often as she could, especially after she retired."

"What did she do before she retired?"

"Mostly social work, in different places. She was always helping someone, it seemed. I could count on her to make time for me when I was here, though. She taught me a lot about the natural environment."

"I guess they were alike in that way, your aunt and my uncle. Helping other people, you know, caring. Uncle Miguel never married and didn't have any kids of his own, and I think I was his favorite nephew. Probably because I wanted to be just like him."

"And were you? Just like him?"

"Somewhat, I like to think."

"Tell me more about him."

"Always busy. Interested in people. He grew up speaking French, Spanish, and English. Later he added a little Italian and Portuguese. Languages came easily to him. And he fit in wherever he went. People just seemed to welcome him because he not only spoke their language but adopted the mannerisms of their culture."

"He sounds great."

"Yeah, he was."

"You miss him a lot."

"I do. I was with him when he was dying, and he made me promise not to spend too much time grieving. Instead, he wanted me to go on and enjoy my life. He said we all die, and it's hard for those left behind. But life goes on. I thought that was an amazing gift he gave me. I still grieve, but I try to keep his upbeat look on life with me wherever I go."

"That is a gift."

When they reach the top of the hill, Brent stares out at the dark blue water rippling toward shore far below them. "Wow. What a view! Almost like looking out at the ocean."

"No salt is all."

"Right." He smiles at her. A warm and beautiful smile, she thinks.

"What are those islands?" He points to the two islands straight out from the bluff where they stand. The islands look close together, similar but with different sandy bluffs that stand out clearly against the cloudless blue sky.

"The Manitous. The Indigenous people describe them as two bear cubs who drowned. And that sand dune over there is their mother, watching out for them." She points it out.

"Good story to explain the land formations."

"And maybe a story about the connection of people in families. Are you hungry?"

"Definitely."

They sit on the bench that overlooks the water. Tara is aware of how close he is. It feels comfortable, natural.

"And I brought cookies from the bakery."

"What kind?"

"A few different ones. I wasn't sure what kind you like."

Tara is pleased that he considered what she might like. She unpacks the sandwiches and hands him one.

"Thanks." Brent takes a bite of his sandwich and watches the water below them. "What did your aunt do besides hike? My uncle said she was adventurous, because she went all the way to France by herself, without even other students from her own university."

"She was always up for something new, something to explore. She shared that with me, and we had many fun times together. One spring vacation when I went with them to the Caribbean, we watched someone hang-glide over the ocean. My aunt thought that looked like fun and we should try it. Uncle Robb said no way, he didn't think it was safe. But my aunt checked it out with the people at our resort, and they said the guy who took people out was reliable. I was definitely up for it, so she and I went together. And it was spectacular."

"Were you scared?"

"A bit, yes, but my aunt made me feel perfectly safe."

"Hard to lose someone like that."

"Very. I still grieve, but I realize just how lucky I was to have her in my life, even though it didn't last forever as I wish it had."

Tara changes the subject to keep from crying. She wants to just enjoy this time with Brent. "I never asked you where you are staying."

"I am staying in this small cabin in the woods. A new experience for me. But a friend of mine, Eric, inherited it from his grandfather and he told me I could use it anytime I wanted. He met me up here for a couple of days and when he left, told me to stay as long as I wanted. Since I was coming up here to find your aunt, it seemed like a good idea to stick around a while. The cabin is a bit rustic, but comfortable." He looks at her with his warm, brown eyes.

Tara surprises herself when she wants to say, "stay a long time," but it's definitely too soon. She doesn't know him that well.

"When you were a kid, what did you want to be when you grew up?" Brent looks at her.

"This sounds silly, but I wanted to be a firefighter."

"Really? How come?"

"I had a toy fire truck with a spotted dog sitting on the back. You could take him off and on. I imagined my Dalmatian and me rushing to the fire and being the heroes who save everyone."

"Sounds heroic." He smiles at her. "You changed your mind?"

Tara laughs. "When I grew up, I realized that it's not so easy to be the hero. Fires are dangerous and messy."

"True."

"What about you? What did you want to be?"

"I wanted to be a pirate."

"A pirate?"

"We had a movie about a kid who goes off to be a pirate. He is very good-looking and brave. And of course he becomes rich."

"That does sound like a good job." They both laugh.

"Life changes our dreams and ambitions, doesn't it?" Tara sounds wistful.

"Yeah, I guess it does. But there is always something interesting to do."

"So, is being a lawyer your favorite job ever?"

"It's interesting, but my favorite job was when I was in college."

"Really? What did you do?"

"When I was a sophomore, I decided to stay in the dorm another year. I was a bit lazy, I guess. Meals prepared for me and all that. I had this zany roommate. He was always doing outrageous things that made people laugh. Not harmful things, just unexpected. Like one time when we went to the grocery store to buy a couple of things for a party we were going to, he came walking by with a big haunch of meat slung over his shoulder, like he was a cave man, or something. Totally unexpected, just made me laugh.

I got into the spirit of it, and the two of us ended up as the dorm comedy team. People told us we should go on stage, but that seemed unlikely. We came up with the idea that we could learn some magic tricks and entertain kids at birthday parties."

"Did that work?"

"Definitely. We printed up flyers and business cards and did a couple of demonstrations in public places. It turned out to be a regular thing for weekends, and we expanded a bit into family reunions and other kinds of parties. We made people laugh and they loved it. And we made some needed money."

"Sounds fun. What happened to your zany roommate?"

"He went into advertising."

"And he likes that?"

"Yeah. He's been a big success. You know that milk advertisement where this family is having a picnic and a bear shows up? The family panics, but then the bear asks if they have any milk and cookies. And this adorbs little kid hands the bear his glass of milk and his cookie."

"That's pretty funny."

"That's his ad. It's one of the most favorite ads out there."

"He found what he is really good at doing. And can make money doing it."

"What about you? Favorite job?"

"One summer I worked at an ice cream shop by the beach. I didn't really like serving ice cream, but I made a couple of good friends who worked there. After work we always put on our suits and went down to the beach. Of course, there were always teenage guys around."

"Ah, I see." He grins at her.

They hear voices from people coming up the path.

"We should probably move on." Tara stands up.

Brent picks up the backpack. "This feels a bit heavy."

"Oh, I almost forgot about the stones."

"Like stone soup?"

Tara laughs. "No, I missed Aunt Becca's memorial service because I had Covid. And I found a box of stones that she had picked up over the years. I have been hiking to her favorite places and building small cairns in her memory. A closure kind of thing." She looks at him. "Corny?"

"No, of course not. Sounds like a great idea. This was one of her favorite hikes?"

Tara nods. She takes out the stones she has chosen and builds a small cairn underneath a tree on the bluff overlooking the Lake.

"I always say a few words." She looks up to see if he thinks that's weird.

"Nice. Do you want me to walk away so you can do that?"

Tara gives him a grateful smile. "No, you can stay."

"In memory of Aunt Rebecca. You made life seem full of adventures and encouraged me to be open to that. I haven't had as many adventures as I would like. I'm going to focus more on that in the near future."

"Sounds like a good plan." She looks up. He is smiling at her.

Walking down the main path, they meet a group of four coming up the hill. Everyone exchanges a hello, nice day for a hike, and Tara and Brent turn left.

At an intersection of the trail, Tara points to the sign. "To the right is a trail straight down the hill back to the parking lot. That way to the left goes on to another lake, Glen Lake. Have you had enough or want to go on?"

"Another lake? I'm all for it."

They continue on the trail until Tara stops and points behind them toward the view of Lake Michigan and the coastline curving around it.

"Nice!"

The trail goes up hill and down, trees and bushes crowding against the sides of it. A short trail off to the left leads to a bluff overlooking Glen Lake.

Brent looks out at the smooth expanse of deep blue water fading into aqua along the shoreline. "Another fine view. This is definitely the land of lakes."

"I always loved coming up here to visit my aunt and uncle. The water is never far away."

They sit close together on the bench.

"You didn't grow up around here?"

"I did, sort of. My parents are divorced and both remarried. I spent most of the summers up here with my aunt and uncle."

"Siblings?"

"When my mom remarried, I inherited two step-brothers, Ian who was nine and Jordan who was eleven. I was 10 when my mom remarried, and the two brothers went back and forth between their mom and dad. That felt a bit chaotic to me. They were with us one week and we were getting to know each other, and then they were gone the next week and it was just the three of us. Suddenly, on the weekends when they stayed with us to be with their dad, I was a middle child. And when they were with their mom, I was an only child. I found it very confusing.

"When my dad remarried, I suddenly became the oldest child in his family, and my dad and stepmom wanted me to adore my little step-sister Chelsea, who was only one year old. My dad and stepmom had a child together, who is my half-sister, Riley. When she was born, I was the eldest sister to two younger kids. At first, I just found them annoying, but they were both cute and smart. They looked up to me, and I enjoyed playing with them and teaching them how to do things. By the time my half-sister was born, though, I was already a teenager and busy with my own stuff. I wasn't really around much after I turned eighteen, so they grew up a lot without me. I've kept in touch with both of them.

"Jordan was one of those super athletes who could be a star at any sport he tried. My stepdad was really into that. My younger brother, Ian, was more the musical/artsy type. It was hard for him to fit in, because Jordan got a lot of the attention. So, Ian and I became really close. A couple of years ago he came out to me, and that made us closer than ever. I said I would support him if he decided to come out to my mom and stepdad. But he wasn't ready to test that back then. He moved to Portland, Oregon, I think to get away from family dynamics, and I visited him in Portland a couple of times. We kept in touch, and he came here to visit this summer. I was proud of him for finally coming out to my mom and stepdad. When he was here, he suggested I move out there. I'm considering it."

"Sounds like a complicated family life. Would you, do you think, move out to Portland?"

Tara shrugs. "Maybe. Still trying to decide which direction to go."

Brent gives her a long look. "Staying with your aunt and uncle was a relief, in a way?"

"Yes. You? Intact family? Siblings?"

"Yes, to both. I was lucky, I guess. My parents both had professional jobs and were often busy, but they found time for us. I have two sisters, one who is older and lives in Colorado and one younger who lives in Washington, D.C."

"Were you close with your sisters growing up?"

"Sometimes. Depended on our ages at different times. Since I was the only boy and the child in the middle, I sometimes ended up being the peacemaker between my sisters when they fought. But other times, they ganged up on me a bit. We always looked out for each other, though. And as adults we get along pretty well."

"It must be nice to have siblings that you grew up with like that."

"It is. I'm lucky, I guess."

They walk back on the trail to the intersection and follow the sign that points toward the parking lot. They walk without speaking, in a comfortable silence.

"Okay, this is downhill. How hard can it be?" He grabs her hand and starts to run. Brent slows them down before they trip over their own feet. At the bottom, they both stop and burst out laughing. They don't let go of each other's hand.

That night before she turns out the light, Tara texts her friend. "I think I've met someone."

"What do you mean YOU THINK? Either you met him or you didn't."

"Ha, ha. I've only known him for a week. But when we're together, I feel like the sun just came out on a cloudy day. And there is a definite spark between us."

"Sounds like you've MET someone!"

"But I thought Kyle was the one for a while. And he wasn't."

"Know what they say. No pain, no gain. Kyle was the pain. This guy might be the gain part. He have a name?"

"Brent."

"Good name. I say go for it. You only live once and all that. What do you have to lose but your sanity?"

"Ha, ha. I'll let you know."

Thirty

The morning of Maria's birthday, Tara and Uncle Robb take Maria to the rehab center to see her grandma. Sitting in a comfortable chair in the lounge, she smiles when they walk in. Maria hugs her grandma and hands her a bouquet of stargazer lilies, her grandma's favorite.

"Happy birthday, Maria," her grandma says. She slurs the words just a little, but is clearly pleased to be able to say it. "Thank you for the flowers." Grandma hands her a present that she asked a friend to buy for her.

"Thank you for the present."

"Open."

Maria carefully unwraps the shiny wrapping paper and unfolds the tissue paper that surrounds the gift. The framed picture of her with her mother, sister, and Grandma in front of her grandma's garden brings tears to her eyes. She murmurs a thank you and sets the picture up next to the flowers.

Tara unpacks the cake with plates and silverware. She cuts pieces for the nurses and other people in the lounge who look over with eager eyes. Uncle Robb starts singing Happy Birthday, and everyone joins in. Maria smiles.

Tara and Uncle Robb start a conversation with two of the rehab patients while they eat cake. Maria and her grandma speak Spanish, a language that is comforting to both of them.

"I will be able to go home at the end of the week." Grandma tells Maria.

"You will finally be home. I hated thinking of you here alone. I'll take good care of you." Maria's eyes are wide.

"Don't worry. I am doing okay and can take care of myself with just a little help." She hugs Maria.

"We have made arrangements for a nurse to stop by every other day to check on Grandma's progress and to continue occupational therapy, as needed. Also, there are other helpers who can come to assist. You both just need to let us know." The nurse pats Grandma's shoulder. "We will miss one of our favorite patients."

On the way home, Robb looks in the rearview mirror at Maria in the back seat. "How do you feel about your grandma coming home?"

"I am so glad that she is okay and can go home." Maria is quiet for a minute. "But I will miss you and Tara and Taffy."

"You aren't losing us. You are welcome to come over often, and we will visit you and your grandma."

Maria nods. "Grandma says when she is all well, we can think about getting a dog. She says I'm always saying Taffy this and Taffy that. It can't be a puppy, though, because Grandma doesn't want to house train her. You got Taffy when she was older, right? Already house-trained and all."

"Yes, she was about a year old, I think. The Humane Society always has grown-up dogs who need homes."

"I will give one a home." Maria nods with satisfaction.

"Good for you." Tara smiles.

In the kitchen Uncle Robb looks up from chopping vegetables. "Sounds like Maria will be going back to stay with her grandma in a few days."

"Her grandma is making great progress and is very determined to go home. The rehab center is organizing a visiting nurse to continue her physical exercises and her progress with speech. She should be able to manage self-care, but may not be able to handle everything."

"We'll miss Maria."

Tara pauses as she whisks the salad dressing. "She has perked us up a bit, I think. We can still see her, though." She looks at her uncle.

"She brought back many happy memories for me. Of happier times. When you spent the summers with Becca and me. Hearing the voices and the laughter from the hammock always made me smile."

Tara puts her arm around her uncle and hugs him. "For me, too."

"I will probably have some time to go over there and help out with a few things."

"That will please Maria, I'm sure. She is very attached to you."

"And her grandma and I have a tally going with gin rummy. I think she has won more games than I have, so I have to even things up."

Maria comes into the kitchen. "Jayden is going to help me to put up the lights outside."

"Sounds good." Uncle Robb takes the lid off the cake carrier and begins to frost the cake. He and Tara gently push fourteen candles into the soft, flaky texture.

Outside, Jayden turns on the lights that are strung up along the roof of the porch. Jayden and Maria blow up balloons and tie them to the porch posts. Hailey, who came over early, grabs one of the balloons and runs around the yard, bumping it up in the air. Taffy joins the game, and nudges the balloon with her nose if it hits the ground.

Uncle Robb starts a fire in the grill while Tara prepares the picnic table.

"Maria, come meet a couple of my friends," Jayden calls out as he walks with a boy and a girl across the backyard toward Maria. "This is Gavin. He's a mean hitter on the Sonics, more home runs than anyone else." He gently punches Gavin's arm.

"Hi. Jayden is not such a shabby hitter himself."

"I'm Kyla. I'm not on their team, but I'm here, too." Kyla shakes her head at Jayden and Gavin and hands Maria a small present. "Happy Birthday, from all of us."

"Thanks." Maria takes the present and smiles. "There are drinks and snacks on the table."

Gavin and Jayden pile up their plates. Kyla smiles at Maria and rolls her eyes as she puts cheese, crackers, and vegetables on her plate.

Jayden's mom and his older sister Lauren arrive with Lauren's friend, Madison, and Madison's little sister, Maya, who runs over to play with Hailey.

"Glad you all could come to help us celebrate." Robb walks over to Jayden's mom, wiping his hands on an apron. "Just got the fire going."

"Jayden talks a lot about Maria. He knows what it's like to lose someone and not have them around." Her smile fades as she takes a deep breath. "I'm glad they have become friends."

"Jayden has been good for Maria. She seems more confident, happier. She is a breath of fresh air for me, but hanging out with an old guy is probably a bit boring for her."

Jayden's mom laughs. "You could never be boring, Robb."

The neighborhood is quiet, but every time a car passes by the house, Tara looks up to see who it is. When the car she is waiting for pulls into the driveway, Tara smiles and walks over to meet the driver. Brent gets out of the car and takes a present out of the back seat.

"You made it."

"Wouldn't miss it. A chance to wish Maria happy birthday. And a chance to see you again."

"Both good things to do." She hugs him and he hugs her back.

Maria takes Brent over to Maria and her friends, and Brent hands her a small box wrapped in colorful flowered paper. "Happy Birthday."

"Thanks."

"Go ahead, open it." Jayden nudges Maria's arm.

She carefully takes off the paper, opens up the box, and takes out a small replica of a red, blue, and green piñata. She gives Brent a big smile. "A piñata. Just like we would have at home. Only smaller."

"It actually does have candy in it, but there is a door in the bottom, so you can open it instead of hitting it with a stick."

Maria finds the door in the piñata, opens it, and pours several pieces of candy into her hand. She laughs and passes candy around.

Tara smiles. "Great present."

At the end of the party, Brent and Maria start to clear the table while Tara and Robb put the leftovers away. Maria looks up shyly at Brent.

"Do people ever say mean things to you because you have a Spanish last name?"

"It has happened on occasion."

"Does it make you mad?"

"It does, definitely. But I try to ignore it. Well, most of the time. I actually almost got into a big fight when this guy my friend and I were playing basketball with at the park called me a spic. I pushed him, he pushed me back, and we both raised our fists. Fortunately, my friend said the guy wasn't worth the trouble and pulled me back."

"What's a spic?"

"It's a slur against Italians, so he didn't really know where I am from."

"Are you a citizen of the United States?" Maria sets down the plates she is holding.

"Yes, I am. My mother was born in Chicago, so I was lucky to be born here. And my dad's family lived in California for many generations. I know it isn't easy for people who immigrate here these days. I am sorry about what happened to your mother and sister."

Maria nods, but is quiet. Brent pats her shoulder, and they carry the dishes inside.

Later that night Maria comes into Tara's room. "Thanks for the party. I really missed my mom and sister being here, but I texted them pictures. They are very happy for me. And my mom said muchas gracias to you and Uncle Robb." She wipes away a tear.

Tara pats the bed beside her and Maria sits close to her. "I'm so sorry they couldn't be here." She puts an arm around Maria and Maria leans against her.

After a few moments Maria looks up at Tara. "That guy who came to my party, Brent. Is he your boyfriend? He's pretty hot."

Tara laughs. "I think he's hot, too. I think he might be my boyfriend."

Thirty-one

"Are you okay if Brent and I go out to his cabin this evening?" Tara feels guilty that she has agreed to this. She's the one who brought both Taffy and Maria into her uncle's life, and she shouldn't rely on him to take care of them.

"Of course. You don't have to babysit me. I'll be okay. A bit of quiet time won't hurt. Not that it's ever totally quiet with Maria around." He smiles as if that isn't a bad thing.

"I'll leave Taffy here to keep you company, too, if that's okay."

"No problem."

Brent steers the car down a dirt road with pine trees lined up on either side. "Not much of a road but it's nice and quiet out here."

Through the woods, Tara glimpses wildflowers gleaming in the sun that splashes down through the pine boughs. Brent drives the car into a cleared space on the edge of the road and gestures toward a path into the woods.

"Just a short walk down that way."

They walk close together down the narrow trail, and Miguel takes her hand. The path ends by a log cabin nestled among the pine trees. There is a green door in the middle of a small front porch, with a window on either side of it.

"This is it. It's small but works for me." He opens the door and sets down the backpack and cooler he has been carrying.

Tara looks around at the comfortable-looking plaid couch and the two mismatched chairs before the fireplace on one side of the main room. A large, round oak table with four chairs sits in the corner beside a sink, a stove, a small old-fashioned refrigerator, and a few cupboards. Down a short hallway, there is a bathroom and a bedroom. A sloping ladder leads up to a loft with four more beds and a large chest of drawers.

"Looks like a hunting cabin."

"That's what it's mostly used for. There is a patio out the back door. With some chairs and a grill. Thought I would make my famous shrimp shish kebabs for dinner." He smiles at her.

"Famous, huh?"

"Definitely. Friends often ask me to fix them." He smiles at her and lifts his eyebrows.

"Must be we're friends then." She smiles back.

Tara makes a salad while Brent marinates the kebabs. Then she sits on the patio and watches Brent cook, basting and turning the kebabs while talking with her. The light in the woods washes the trees in a pale gold as the sun starts to go down. They sit at the patio table and savor the salad and kebabs, pausing to talk about their childhoods, vacations they have taken, favorite things.

When the mosquitoes come out and buzz around their heads, they quickly grab everything and take it into the cabin. The air starts to cool off, and together they build a fire in the fireplace. They sit on the lumpy couch and watch the orange and yellow flames shoot upwards. Brent puts his arm around her and pulls her close. She turns her face to look at him and he kisses her. She puts her arms around him, and the kiss deepens. A few minutes later, he pulls away and looks at her.

She takes his hand to pull him up and leads him to the bedroom. Slowly, they begin to explore each other's bodies and discover what feels good. Afterward, they pull up the covers and snuggle underneath, their bodies touching length to length.

"You are so beautiful, physically of course, but also as a person," he says as he kisses her cheek.

"I feel the same about you," she says and kisses him again.

They lie curled up together, and soon Brent drifts off to sleep. Out the bedroom window Tara watches the sliver moon in the night sky cast a faint glow on the pine trees. Ian is right. It's time to move on. Not to forget, but to forge ahead.

When she wakes in the morning, Brent is up and she smells coffee brewing. For a few minutes she watches out the window as the dim light sifts through the trees. The birds are already up, and she listens carefully to see how many different songs she can identify. She stretches and smiles.

"Good morning." Brent wraps his arms around her, and she relaxes into the solidness of him. "What do you want for breakfast? We have eggs and toast, and I found flour and maple syrup if you want pancakes."

"Eggs and toast would be a luxury. I don't usually eat more than toast."

When they have finished breakfast, Tara helps him to clean up the kitchen.

"What do you think about going for a hike this morning? There is a trail from the cabin out to some of the main trails that go through the woods."

"I'd like to see more of the woods."

The trail leads deeper into the trees, and they cross a short bridge over a narrow creek. They listen to the gurgles of the creek and let the soft, warm breeze caress their faces. Tara turns her face toward the sun and closes her eyes. Brent leans down and kisses her.

"I wasn't sure if I was doing the right thing to come all this way and deliver my uncle's letter to your aunt. But it turned out to be one of the best things I ever did." He looks into her eyes and she knows he is talking about her.

"I'm glad you decided to come. When I was reading the journals and later your uncle's letters to my aunt after she came back to the States, I felt really connected to their story. But I didn't know about you. You make it my story, too."

At a junction in the trail, a sign points toward a lake at the bottom of a hill and they follow a trail down to a small, round lake surrounded by evergreens. They sit on one end of a log that fell into the creek long ago and talk about some of the things they each hope to do in the future.

"Do you like to sail? All these lakes remind me of the times I used to go sailing a lot, when we lived in Chicago. My dad had a big sailboat back then, and we used to do the Chicago to Mackinac race. I still keep a small sailboat at my parents' house."

"I sailed once with a kid I met here one time when I was staying with my aunt and uncle. I really enjoyed it, and I planned to buy a sailboat one day and sail all around the world." She laughs.

"Still time for that, you know." He grins.

At the end of the afternoon Brent drives Tara back to her uncle's house and walks her to the door.

"I have to go back to Detroit for a few days. I have been keeping up with much of the paperwork required of a lawyer, but there are meetings I that I have to attend. He looks at her, and she is not sure what he is thinking."

"Oh. Hope all that goes well for you." She looks away. Is this his way of saying goodbye? Just a fling after all?

"I'll be back as soon as I can." He turns her towards him and looks into her eyes. "As soon as." He puts his arms around her and kisses her. She leans into him and kisses him back, wants to believe that he really will be back. She has to trust that he will. The thought of not seeing him again leaves her feeling hollow. How did he come to mean so much to her so quickly?

That evening Tara feels restless. After dinner she and Uncle Robb sit on the back porch. The air feels oppressive, heavy with moisture. They watch dark clouds move across the sky in their direction. Within a few minutes, raindrops splat onto the porch. They hurry inside as rain pours down, dripping off the roof.

Thirty-two

Tara comes home to a quiet house. Uncle Robb's car is gone, and there is no note on the table by the front door where her aunt and uncle always left messages if they had gone somewhere. Uncle Robb is a bit forgetful since her aunt died. Maybe he just forgot what time she usually comes home from work.

She changes her clothes and puts some laundry in the washer. Then she takes the book she is reading and sits on the back porch. After a busy day waiting on all the tourists, she could use a quiet time to read and think.

In the backyard the trees and grass have exploded into a vibrant green after last night's rain. Peas and beans shoot up in the vegetable garden, and a few tiny green tomatoes appear on their plants. Along the side of the yard, the row of peony blossoms burst in a display of white, pink, and red.

What should she do now that Uncle Robb is managing his grief and putting his life back together? What is she good at that could turn into a job? She would love to be a famous novelist, but that is a definite long shot. At one time she thought she might be an intrepid journalist. What about her ecology minor?

She hears the car pull into the driveway. Her uncle says something to Maria, who answers with an anxious voice, and the front door closes. Tara puts down her book and goes in-

side. Her uncle and Maria stand in the hallway, and he seems
to be trying to comfort her.

"Is something wrong?"

Maria turns and sees Tara. "I'm sorry. I don't know if I
shut the gate all the way or not."

"What's happened? Is it your grandma?" Tara frowns,
puzzled. What does that have to do with the gate?

Uncle Robb shakes his head. He looks so worried that
Tara is alarmed.

"What's happened?"

"It's the dog."

"Taffy? Where is she?"

"We can't find her."

"What do you mean?"

"Taffy was restless, pacing around the house. She sometimes does that when you are gone. I thought it would be
okay to let her out in the yard on her own. But I didn't check
the gate. It's always latched, but there have been so many
people in and out lately." Uncle Robb shakes his head. "I'm so
sorry. I know how much she means to you. We'll find her. I've
been out looking, but no luck so far."

"How long has she been gone?"

"I'm not sure. An hour maybe." He frowns.

Tara's eyes fill with tears. "She could have been hit by a
car. Do you think she's dead?"

"No, no, not that." Uncle Robb comes to her quickly and
puts his arms around her. "I'm sure she's okay. Just enjoying a
good run probably."

"What does Maria have to do with it?"

"Nothing really. She's convinced she forgot to latch the
gate, and that's how Taffy got out. I told her we don't know
who forgot."

Tara finds she is shaking. She heads for the door. "I have
to find her."

"I'm going to go see if Jayden can help us look. We can ask all the neighbors if they've seen her." Without waiting for an answer, Maria dashes out the door and down the street.

Uncle Robb follows Tara out the door. She walks up one side of the street and he walks up the other side. When they reach the end of the street, Tara heads into the neighborhood woods, a likely place Taffy would explore. She follows the loop trail to the left, and Robb follows the loop to the right.

"Taffy! Where are you? Come!" Tara spins in all directions, stops and listens for sounds of thrashing through the trees. All is silent except for a squirrel who scurries along a downed log and a chickadee who calls, "Dee, dee, dee." She follows the short trail through the woods and emerges onto another street. No Taffy. Walking from house to house, she asks people if they have seen her dog. No one has seen her. Taffy is her companion. What will she do if she can't find her?

Finally, Uncle Robb catches up with her. "Come on. Let's go home and make some flyers. We'll post them everywhere. Someone will have seen her. Maybe she's already at home."

Tara looks at him, hopefully. "Yes. She would return home when she's done roaming." She heads back through the woods, trying not to think that maybe Taffy was hit by a car, that she is lying in the street somewhere. Maybe she will never see her dog again.

When they get home, Taffy isn't there. Tara finds a photo of Taffy on her phone, and together they design a poster about a missing dog. Robb prints up several copies and hands some of them to Tara.

Maria runs into the house with Jayden, Lauren, and Hailey right behind her. "Tara, we might have found her."

"Where?" Tara jumps up.

"Mr. Macintosh down the street says he saw a brown and white dog run into the yard behind his just a few minutes ago."

"Show me."

They race down the street and around the corner to a two-story white house with a small yard in front and a large back-yard. They pass a small flower garden with two plastic chairs beside it.

"He said we can go through his yard to look back there." Tara takes off running. Behind the house they spread out, calling Taffy's name.

"I need to talk to Mr. Macintosh." Tara dashes back to the white house and up the porch steps. Before she knocks a gray-haired man comes to the door.

"You must be Tara."

Tara nods. "Please tell me about the dog that you saw. Was she hurt?"

"No, she looked okay."

"How big was she?"

"About so high." He places his palm out to just above his knees.

Tara nods. Could be Taffy. "Did she have a tail?"

"It was a thin tail, black, I think."

Tara frowns. That doesn't sound like Taffy. "What was her fur like? Long, short, curly, straight?"

"Short and straight, I think."

Tara's shoulders slump, and tears come into her eyes. False alarm. "Thanks." She walks to the sidewalk where the rest of them wait.

"Not Taffy. The description is wrong."

"I'm sorry. He said brown and white."

Uncle Robb fixes a simple dinner, but none of them eat much. Tara pushes her food around on her plate, then stands up and goes out onto the front porch. She walks up one side of the street and down the other side, looking for Taffy, call-ing her name. Finally, giving up, she comes inside and goes up to her room.

Maria stands in the doorway. Tara doesn't look up, lost in her own thoughts.

"I'm sorry, Tara. Maybe I didn't latch the gate tightly."

"It's not your fault. It could have been anyone." Right now, Tara blames everyone who walked through that gate today. All she can manage is, "We'll find her," because she can't bear the thought that Taffy is gone.

"I know we will." Maria sighs and walks down the hall to her own room.

Tara wonders what Brent is doing. She had decided not to text him while he was gone, not wanting to seem needy. She looks at her phone, finds his number, puts her phone down, lies back on the bed. Then she picks up the phone and sends a text, "Taffy is missing. We can't find her anywhere." Within minutes the response comes, "I'll be there tomorrow to help you look. We'll find her."

Tara lies in bed and stares out the window at the gray darkness. Taffy is out there alone somewhere in the dark. Is she hurt? Unable to find her way home? Tara leaves the curtains open, as if that will help Taffy find her way home. A sliver of moonlight slices the floor, and she watches it move slowly across the room. She closes her eyes but is not able to sleep. If she doesn't find Taffy, will she get another dog? There is no other dog that will do.

Tara feels she hasn't been asleep long when she hears a tap, tap, tap on the front door. It is not a loud sound, but it is insistent. A dim light sifts through the window, not quite dawn. She gets up, pulls on her robe, and hurries down the stairs. When she opens the door, she is not sure what surprises her the most. Brent stands on the porch with a big smile on his face. Even more surprising is that Taffy lies beside him with her head on her paws. As Tara kneels down, Taffy stands up and nudges into her arms, almost knocking her over. Tara puts her arms around the dog and chokes back tears.

"Taffy, where have you been?" Taffy licks Tara's face. "Why is your fur all dirty?"

"Is that an indication of which of us is most welcome this morning?" Brent pretends to look hurt, but she can see that he is delighted. "Told you we'd find her."

Laughing, Tara stands up and gives Brent a fierce hug. "You are so welcome. More than you can know. I should give Taffy some water and food, while you tell me how you and Taffy came to be here."

Taffy quickly slurps up the water that Tara pours into her bowl and wolfs down the food Tara dumps into her dish. Brent sits at the kitchen table and watches them. When she is sure Taffy is well cared for, Tara sits down across from him.

"So, what's your story? Do you have some kind of magic that I didn't know about?" She can't stop beaming.

"Afraid I was just lucky. I left really early this morning because I was worried about you, and Taffy. When I got here, I waited in the car because I realized you were probably all asleep. Suddenly, I saw Taffy walking slowly down the sidewalk. I got out of the car and she limped up to me and nudged my hand."

"That's amazing. I am so glad you came to help me look for her." She reaches across the table and takes his hand. "It feels like magic."

While Tara is upstairs getting dressed, Uncle Robb comes into the kitchen. He rubs his eyes when he sees Brent at the kitchen table drinking a cup of coffee, Taffy lying at his feet.

"Am I seeing things?"

"No, we're for real." Brent again explains how he came to be there and find Taffy.

Maria stands in the door, her eyes wide. "You found her." She hesitates. Taffy stands up and goes over to her. Tears come into Maria's eyes as she pets the dog's head.

"Come, sit down. I'll get you some juice." Uncle Robb looks at her kindly.

"You are surprised to see both of us, I bet." Brent explains for the third time how he came to be here, how he found Taffy or rather Taffy found him.

After breakfast Tara and Brent put Taffy into the bathtub and give her a bath. Tara gently feels the dog's paws. The right front one seems tender, but there is no apparent injury. Maria rubs the dog with a towel and they take her outside to dry off. Taffy lets out a sigh, lies down in the sun, and goes to sleep.

"What do you think happened to her?" Maria looks at Tara.

"I don't know." Tara pauses. "Maybe she was abducted by kidnappers who planned to ransom her for a large sum of money. Or, they had seen her playing ball and thought they could get rich by entering her in competitions where she would win. They locked her up somewhere, but she escaped and found her way home."

"Or maybe she entered another universe or time traveled to the past. And she missed us, so she found the entryway to get back here." Maria laughs.

Brent thinks for a moment. "Maybe she was on a rescue mission because she is a guard dog for an important person, and she had to find him because he works for some spy agency." Tara rolls her eyes, but grins at him.

"Or, maybe she saw a unicorn and chased after it into the woods where a magician put a magic spell on her, but the unicorn helped her find her way home." Uncle Robb looks over at Taffy.

"Good one, Uncle Robb."

Thirty-three

As Tara passes Maria's room, she sees Maria sitting on the bed, staring out the window. Maria looks up when Tara knocks on the door casing.

"Are you excited that your grandma is going home today?"

Maria shrugs. "I am happy that she has recovered enough to go home. But I am happy here."

"We are happy to have you here. But you aren't going far away. Maybe you should leave a few of your things here. You can come back whenever you want to."

"Do you think that would be okay?"

"More than okay. It will help Uncle Robb remember that you aren't leaving for good. He will be happy to know you will be back."

"I will still see both of you, won't I?"

Tara puts her arm around Maria. "Of course. We wouldn't let you get away."

"Okay." Maria smiles. "That kind of makes me sound like a fish."

Tara laughs. "A keeper anyway. We should get going soon to pick up your grandma."

Tara goes downstairs. Uncle Robb is busy making breakfast. Taffy lies by the open kitchen door.

"She ready?"

"Mostly. Feeling sad about leaving."

"Me, too. But we will still see her."

After breakfast they drive to the rehab center. Maria's grandma hugs her with a big smile on her face. She shakes hands with Robb and Tara and thanks them over and over for all they have done for her and Maria. There is paperwork to fill out and lots of instructions about what to expect and exercises to continue when she is home. Grandma insists that she is capable of walking out of the hospital, but the nurse gently helps her settle into a wheelchair. Maria wheels her grandma out to the pick-up point where Uncle Robb waits with the car. Tara carries the walker and her grandma's possessions.

At the house, Grandma eases out of the car, looks at the house and flowers, and sighs with contentment. She is home.

"Uncle Robb and I cleaned the house and bought groceries," Maria says proudly and gestures around with her arm.

Grandma has tears in her eyes as she looks around her home, and thanks all of them. Maria hugs Uncle Robb and Tara.

"Don't worry. We are still here for you. I'll be coming over with meals now and then. And to win back my reputation at gin rummy." Uncle Robb smiles at Grandma.

"And you have to finish the book."

"What book?" Tara looks at her uncle.

"Uncle Robb and Grandma are reading The Long Petal of the Sea."

"Grandma said she had been wanting to read that, and I had not read it yet, so we decided to read it together."

Tara remembers that her aunt and uncle used to read to each other sometimes. She raises her eyebrows.

Uncle Robb laughs. "No, Grandma and I are not romantically interested in each other. We are friends. I lost Becca and she lost her husband, so we are widower and widow. We each lost someone who can never be replaced."

"Sounds like a great friendship." Tara hugs him.

Sitting in the car on the way home, Tara looks over at him. He looks at ease, perhaps already making plans for future meals he will cook for Maria and her grandma, and walks they can take to help her grandma get exercise. He seems to have taken an interest in Maria and her grandma and be moving forward with his life. It is time for her to move on with her own life.

In the late afternoon Tara and Brent walk barefoot along the beach, carrying their sandals and splashing gently through the cool water. Sun peeks through clouds that drift by in the sky, so that the water is shadowed one moment and sparkling another. Tara hesitates to bring up the fact that Brent will be leaving.

Brent stops and looks at her. "Have you thought about what you want to do now that your uncle seems to be doing fine?"

"I think I want to become a naturalist of some kind. I want to do something useful. Being in nature helped me through my grief. Aunt Becca taught me how to identify plants and trees and birds. She loved being in nature, and I realized that it's important to me as well. I want to teach people to appreciate the natural environment and do something meaningful about climate change."

"You would be great at it. Any idea how you might get there?" He squeezes her hand.

"I looked into a couple of programs, and I know I will have to take some additional classes. I'm thinking ecology and botany as a combination. Maybe some work in other countries, studying flora and fauna elsewhere as well as here. Maybe use my English background to do some writing."

"A friend of mine is a naturalist in Costa Rica. I could put you in touch with him."

"That'd be great."

He leans down and kisses her. "I challenge you to a stone-skipping contest."

"I suppose this is something you are an expert at?"

"Maybe. My uncle taught me when I was about eleven, and I practiced over and over until I could get the stone to skip several times. How about you?"

"Uncle Robb taught me when I was ten."

Brent laughs. "Well, an expert then."

"Probably not an expert, but I'll give it my best."

They saunter along the shoreline, heads down, searching for the perfect stones. Tara picks up one and enjoys the round, smooth feel of it. It looks about the right size. She puts it in her pocket and continues to look along the shore. When she has a few chosen stones, she stops.

"Find what you want?"

"I think so. You start." Brent nods at Tara.

She turns slightly to the side, positions the stone in her hand, snaps her wrist as she lets go of it. The stone skips once, twice, three, four times.

"Not bad." Brent gets into position and tosses his stone. It skips once, twice, three, four times.

"A tie!" Tara turns to him and they shake hands. "And the two champions are…"

Brent pulls her toward him and looks into her eyes. "I'm thinking I need to go to Costa Rica and check out the house that my uncle left to me. Things have been so busy that I haven't really been there since he died. I have to decide what to do with it." Brent pauses and lets out a long breath. Before she can respond, he goes on. "I could introduce you to my naturalist friend."

"Are you thinking I am going with you? Did you offer your friend up as an enticement?"

"Not exactly, but I thought it would help if I gave you two reasons to come. Me, for one of course, and my friend as an extra enticement."

Tara laughs. "You don't need a second enticement."

"So, will you? Come with me? I think your uncle will take care of Taffy. They seem pretty bonded."

Tara thinks about it, decides not to overthink it. It's just a trip to Costa Rica, but a trip with possibilities. "Yes. I would love to go to Costa Rica with you." She puts her arms around him and kisses him with a long, slow kiss.

Acknowledgments

The trails Tara hikes in *Lost and Found* are real trails in northern Michigan. Alligator Hill is the real name of that trail, but the farm trail and the lake trail names have been changed, so I did not have to be totally accurate about them. For example, the farm house on the farm trail is a real house, but is not exactly like it is described in the story.

Most of the events in the 1971 journal are based on real events, but the characters and their personal lives are created by the author and not meant to portray real people.

I wish to thank everyone who encouraged me to continue my writing and who helped in the publication of this book.

The Washtenaw Interfaith Coalition for Immigration Rights from which I learned more about immigration laws and the impact of family separations through deportations. And to attorney Brad Thomson for his compassion and dedication in defending immigrant rights.

The Books and More group for inviting me to discuss *Bear Me in Mind* with them and encouraging me to continue writing: Carol Boosterling, Dianne Gotelare, Gloria O'Neill, Grace Stevick, Joyce Girdis, Leslie Scott, Lori Welzbacker, and Mary Yamamoto.

The members of my writers' group, Chris Thelen, Debbie Smith, and Jill Fenton for helping me to improve the description of the book and for sharing their writing experiences.

Adele Brinkley at With Pen in Hand and Kourtney Schmiedeke at Heartfelt Editorial Services, LLC, for their helpful editorial critiques that improved this book.

Melanie Garzonio for her helpful and insightful comments on the books I write and her continued encouragement and friendship. Also, to Dom Garzonio for his encouragement and to Reid and Nico for delightful entertainment.

Briana Chalker for sharing her artistic vision in the beautiful cover design and just for being Briana.

All the readers who have read my previous books and those who are reading this one.

And always thanks to Peter Solenberger for his technical expertise that made this book possible, his continued support for my writing, and the fun times we share.

Book Group Questions

In *Lost and Found* loss and grief are central themes.

1. What losses/griefs were experienced by each of the characters?

2. How did each character respond to his or her loss/grief?

3. In what ways did the characters help each other to deal with loss or grief?

4. What advice did Miguel give Brent about grief, and how did Brent respond to his grief?

5. What was Rebecca's life like in France in 1971? What was difficult about it? What was rewarding? What was her life like later?

6. What were some significant events that happened in 1971? How did those events compare/contrast with events that happened in 2023?

7. Why do you think Rebecca and Miguel's relationship ended?

8. Why did Tara have such a close relationship with her aunt and uncle?

9. How did Tara decide what direction her life should take?

10. Why did Tara and Brent connect so quickly?

11. What was Taffy's significance in the story?

12. How was Maria's family affected by U.S. immigration policies? How did Maria respond to her sense of loss and what helped her to cope with it?

13. What role did nature play in the novel?

14. How was Uncle Robb's garden a metaphor?

About the Author

Dawn Chalker grew up in Northern Michigan. She received a Master's degree from the University of Michigan and a Northern Naturalist Certificate from Northwestern Michigan College. She writes books for adults and kids. She lives with her husband and a frisky cat on the Leelanau Peninsula.

www.ingramcontent.com/pod-product-compliance
Lightning Source LLC
Chambersburg PA
CBHW071552110726
47908CB00007B/2077